Ren and the
Blue Hands

Also by Ellen Phethean

Sauce, The Poetry Virgins
(Bloodaxe Books, 1994)

Wall
(Smokestack Books, 2007)

Breath
(Flambard, 2009, reprinted Red Squirrel Press, 2014)

Portrait of the Quince as an Older Woman
(Red Squirrel Press, 2014)

Ren and the Blue Hands

A Novel

Ellen Phethean

Postbox
PRESS

First published in the UK in 2016 by Postbox Press,
the literary fiction imprint of Red Squirrel Press.
www.redsquirrelpress.com

Cover image and pencil drawing by Tessa Green.

A CIP catalogue record for this book is available
From the British Library.

ISBN: 978 1 910437 55 1

Red Squirrel Press and Postbox Press are committed to
a sustainable future. This book is printed in the UK by
Charlesworth Press using Forest Stewardship Council
certified paper.
www.charlesworth.com

MIX
Paper from
responsible sources
FSC® C016379

For Jane, Judy and Tessa

Contents

From Song of the Blue Hands

In her room sits the Lady high, with hands as white as snow, we stir and sing, our hands are blue, we're Dyers and we're low...

Chapter 1
The Mazards

'Don't run,' Rose snapped.

'Yes, m'Lady, sorry m'Lady.'

She fell into step beside the older woman. Ren had trained hard, her blue hands had faded. She was eager to meet the courtier she was to serve.

In the Hall, Ren stopped to gaze at Lady Lilac who was wearing a lavender dress; she had refined features and dark hair, arresting and proud - the Governor's daughter and Mistress of the Revels. It was a dream come true. Rose pinched her arm, murmuring: 'Remember what I told you.'

* * *

It was a fine May morning as she began her new life as Lilac's maid. From the kitchen she fetched a tray of warm bread rolls and herb tea for them both. She knocked, then carried the tray in and began to set the plates and cups on the table.

Lilac yawned: 'Bring it here. I'll have it in bed.'

'Lady Rose said Ladies never eat in bed.'

Ren blushed deep red. She'd probably just insulted Lilac.

Lilac laughed: 'She won't know.'

Ren put the tray on Lilac's knees and sat at the table to eat her own roll.

Later, as she was brushing Lilac's hair and pinning it into a neat twist, she asked:

'What sewing shall we be doing this morning?'

'Sewing?'

'Lady Rose said that we were to sew between ten and twelve.'

'I'm not fond of sewing.'

'Oh.'

'You may sew; I might read aloud. Would you like that?'

'Yes, my Lady.'

'Good. That's ten to twelve settled.' Lilac laughed again.

Ren considered what she'd been taught by Lady Rose. Lilac was an important woman. She arranged the Island's public celebrations and entertainments, the first woman to hold the post. Yet Lilac didn't behave as she'd been led to believe: only five years older than Ren, her manner was more like a friend. But that was impossible, of course. It was unsettling.

'Lady Rose said...' Ren stopped as Lilac turned to face her:

'Lady Rose is old-fashioned. Her ways are as ancient as the Isles. Just like my father.' Lilac flushed: 'He wants to keep me wrapped in swaddling all my life. I can't bear it! There's a whole world beyond the seas. Do you think all the women in the cosmos do sewing between ten and twelve?!'

Ren blanched and stuttered.

'Does your father insist you only go where and when he tells you?'

Ren paused: 'He's dead.'

'Oh Ren, I'm sorry. Forgive me. What happened?'

'One minute collecting shells and the next: gone. Washed up two weeks later in Bone Cove.'

Lilac shivered: 'What a name.'

'It's where they all end up about that coast. It's the way the sea carries them.' Ren shrugged. 'It's a common danger for Shebblers.'

Lilac took her shoulders, and looked into her eyes:

'I asked for you as my maid, most particularly, because..'

At that moment, a commotion outside the Barrow Hall brought a fanfare of trumpets.

'Ah!' Lilac smiled: 'The theatre troupe from Braymer - wonderful performers. Come for May Day Revels.'

'Will there be swords, or a story of love?' Ren asked.

'A bit of both, I think. Come.'

Down in the Barrow Hall, Ren craned to see five people in bright clothes parade in: a smooth-cheeked boy in a dress of scarlet, with rouge and a wig, followed by three young men in striped outfits of yellow and green, and an imposing man, with a moustache that stuck out wider than his face, his silver hair in a pigtail. His coat was brown linen, floor length, edged with floral brocade.

He bowed: 'We seek an audience with the Governor of these Isles,' he asked in the singsong accent of the Braymer people.

The Governor in his indigo cloak stood forward.

'I'm Lord Almond, Governor of Calico.'

'Sire, I am Monsieur Charlatan, Actor Manager of The Chancellor of Braymer's men, here for the May Revels and Blue Hand Festival.'

The Governor sat back: 'That's my daughter's responsibility.'

He waved a hand and Lilac stepped forward, bringing Ren to stand by her side.

'You're most welcome, gentlemen. And lady.'

The young boy curtsied and laughter rang through the Hall.

'We look forward to your entertainment.'

Charlatan nodded. 'Thank you my Lady.' He bowed again.

The Governor clicked his fingers. 'Grist?'

A short stocky man in a leather jerkin appeared out of the shadows and inclined his head as the Governor spoke a few words. Grist nodded and sloped off.

Two of the performers started flipping and somersaulting. The Governor sat unmoved as Ren and other maids and courtiers gathered round, clapping. Through the crowd the boy dressed as a lady came dancing past Ren,

'Hss.' He whispered: 'Is that your Mistress?' he nodded his head towards Lilac, 'I bring greetings for her.'

He took her hand; a folded paper was pressed into her palm. She looked at him in surprise. Was this another custom Rose hadn't told her about? He winked and danced off, the other actors following him down the Hall and away. Ren gave the paper to Lilac, who raised her eyebrows, then turned to leave, looking over her shoulder to ensure Ren followed.

They hurried along a corridor, up more stairs, through a small door to dark steps winding up until they stepped into a Lookout turret above the Barrow Hall.

Lilac opened up the paper, then showed it to Ren, who read:

I have news. Meet me at Performer's Tent, tonight - B

Lilac took it back: 'This letter was sent from a member of the Mazards.'

'Do they help you with the Revels?'

Lilac shook her head:

'My father gave me that role to keep me quiet. I use my position to organise other things too. Very convenient.' Her eyes flashed.

'Are they performers, the Mazards?'

'Look around.'

Ren clutched the stone parapet: 'I've never been so high.'

'That's where you used to work, isn't it?' Lilac pointed to the Dye Sheds. 'What was it like?'

Ren shook her head. 'You don't want to hear about that, my Lady.'

'Oh, but I do,' Lilac insisted. 'If you could make life easier for the Blue Hands: the Shebblers, the Grinders, the dye girls.' Lilac waved her arm at the view below: 'All the folk of the Islands who help keep the Cloth and Dye Trade going. Would you do it?'

'Of course.'

Lilac leant on the parapet, looking out.

'We've found a way to change the Blue Hands' lives for the better. To change the world!'

Lilac turned and held up the note: 'Are you willing to help?'

'Me?'

'As a Blue Hand you know your way about, can slip in and out of places I could never go. You can be my secret messenger.' Lilac waited, watching her.

Ren was bewildered. In her training, Lady Rose had never mentioned spying or secret errands. She turned away. Her eyes travelled over the harbour and town, drawn to the Dye Sheds again. She pictured Moss, her blue scarred face, leaning over a steaming vat.

'So. Will you?' Lilac grabbed Ren's hands. She nodded. Lady Rose said maids always obey.

Lilac smiled: 'I knew you were the right choice. We'll begin tonight. I have a special errand for you.'

Ren's stomach twisted.

Lilac drew closer to her: 'My father likes to keep tight control of all that goes on in the Isles. Grist is his chief man; he has a network of spies.'

'Do they watch you, my Lady?'

'Oh yes. They don't like those who show disregard for their ancient rules and customs. They suspect me even when I do nothing.' She laughed. 'Whereas no-one will ever question you.' Lilac waved a hand: 'You're used to commoners and Blue Hands. You can pass under noses invisibly. Perfect for a go-between.'

'Lady Rose never taught me how to be invisible.'

Lilac seemed to think Ren was being amusing: 'I'll make a conspirator of you yet.'

Ren looked down at the Dyeing Sheds, dizzied by the long drop.

'Seek out another member of the Mazards, at the performance. Tonight.'

Ren, clinging tight to the parapet, looked back at Lilac:

'What?'

'Meet Bark and bring me his message. He has a pattern inked on his arm: three leaves.'

'Bark.' Ren repeated, her nerves fizzing.

As Ren dressed herself for the evening's entertainment, she stopped and held out her hands remembering how she'd tried to keep them out of sight when she first came to the Barrow Hall. They'd been worker's hands, stained blue, nails edged in dark lines. Now she lifted them up, turned them, gesturing and smiled to herself - Lilac valued her precisely because of her Blue Hand connection! What would her brother think? Vetch had opposed her leaving the Dye Sheds and the Gild, saying:

'Lady's Maid? She'll go off and never come back.'

'Hush,' her mother had said. 'This is a great honour. She'll be safer, move up in the world.'

'She'll think she's too good for the likes of us.'

Ren swore to herself she'd never think that. When Master Greenweed had taught her to read, she learnt quickly, impressing him and she'd sensed she was marked out for a different future, outside the Dye Sheds. Vetch was jealous, he would never understand the excitement and pleasure of discovering a new world of possibilities.

Lilac wore a cloak in blue velvet, her skin pale against its richness and Ren wore her maid's gown, pink as sunrise, and a grey cloak. From the Barrow Hall, they processed west along the cliffs, down to the Dancing Fields. The Governor's retinue were preceded by Guards and standard bearers. People stepped aside to let them through. Lilac and her father travelled in a sedan chair. Lilac smiled and waved at the crowds from the window, the Governor sat back. Ren, walking behind, noticed how Grist always hovered near the Governor's side.

They followed the path crowded with folk from all over the Isles dressed in their best, from the Barrow Porters in their rusty orange jackets to the Dye Girls in clogs and brightly coloured bandannas. Ren looked around, trying to catch sight of Moss. It seemed years ago, not just three months since leaving her friend and the Sheds. The sedan chair was set down under a striped awning with seating reserved for the nobles and officials of the Isle: the Merchant Count Saffron, Master Greenweed Head of the Gild, and others from the Hall, roped off from the rest. Ordinary folk sat on the bank, the grass freshly scythed. All around there was laughter and chatter, the call of the costermonger selling sweetmeats:

'Myrtle figs! One groat a bunch, Myrtle figs!'

The brewing Mistress at her stall cried:

'Amber Ale and Calico Mead, by the jug or by the cup.

Come one, Come all and have a sup!'

A large wooden cart with curtains on three sides formed an enclosed performance space. A skirt of red stuff hid the wheels below. The crowd were jostling and elbowing to create spaces to sit with a good view of the stage.

While the nobles were finding their seats, Lilac hissed to Ren: 'Go now.'

Pulling her cloak close round her dress, Ren slipped away, glancing around, alert for anyone watching her. She mingled with the crowd, following young lads and girls who were pushing to the front. She saw one or two Blue Hands she knew but they turned away without recognition, whereas some of the men stared in open assessment of her. Round behind the stage, she stood and watched people scurrying about, setting up props, carrying costumes and swords. She fumbled with her cloak, gathering courage to take the next step. She recognised Charlatan, reading a script beside a large tent, went to him and whispered:

'Sir, you're one of the performers, aren't you?'

'And what if I am?' His eyes flashed.

She hesitated, trying to choose the right words.

He sighed and turned away.

'Please..' she began. A loud banging on the cart stage interrupted. Ren whispered: 'What's that?'

'The performance will begin in ten minutes. Sometimes I fear you island folk have mist for brains. Art is wasted, wasted!'

'I need to see Bark.'

Charlatan's face became wary: 'Bark?'

'An errand for the Mistress of the Revels.'

He disappeared through the tent flap, she followed and he pointed to a man, aloof and silent, with nut brown skin and dark eyes, his stillness like an aura around him. His foot rested on a box, his elbow lay across his knee. He stared ahead, lost in thought, chewing a stick of liquorice; every now and then he'd spit, sending a splinter of yellow root onto the ground.

She stared at his naked torso, lean and muscled, noticed a small mark on his left forearm: three inky leaves. She had a great urge to touch them. With a jolt, she noted he wore the loose cotton trousers and red bandanna of a Grinder - he must be about the same age as Vetch, although he had the self-assurance of an older man.

She smoothed her skirt, touched her coif to check stray hairs and walked up to him. He turned to her, their eyes met.

'Who do you seek?'

His voice was a rich brown like his skin, and he spoke with an accent unlike any of the other actors. His four words hummed through her as if she were a stringed instrument.

'Bark?' She realised she'd been expecting an old gnarled tree of a man. He had the smooth skin and suppleness of a sapling.

'I am Bark. Yes.' He pronounced it Barrk, his smile was dazzling, his low laugh like rippling silk.

'Are you a Grinder?' she asked. He widened his arms to show off his costume,

'No. I act a part.' He winked at her.

Ren smiled.

'Lady Lilac sent me.'

He became serious, took her arm, led her aside and spoke so close, she could smell his liquorice breath on her cheek:

'Actors' ship The Starfish, ten of the clock tomorrow. I have Azurro.'

Still holding her arm, he led her towards the tent flap, peering out before letting her go. She backed away, stumbling on guy ropes and boxes, unable to pull her eyes from the opening where he'd disappeared. She returned to the nobles' enclosure to stand behind Lilac and whispered the message into her ear.

As the sun dipped below the sea's horizon and dusk muted the colours, a roll on a drum silenced the humming crowd. The drumming stopped, the curtains were drawn aside: another world came into being. Little candles flickered around the square stage; even empty it held magic possibilities. A bird sang somewhere, a trilling of notes. Charlatan strode into the centre of the stage and threw out his arms, calling:

'Welcome to the May Revels! My Lord Governor and nobles. Mistress of the Revels.'

He nodded in the nobles' direction, then he turned to the crowd:

'Welcome to your very own Blue Hands performance.'

A roar went up, and applause.

'People of the Isles of Calico - we crave your indulgence as we perform a Cosmorama, The Cosmos Turned Chaos - a spectacle for your delight.'

A man walked across the stage on his hands, juggling a ball on his feet. Ren's eyes were hooked like tiny fish, nothing could tear her away. She held her breath as Charlatan strode from one end of the cart to the other. He spoke to her, his eyes locked onto her face:

'Tonight, you will witness terrible deeds,' he drew his hand across his throat. She trembled. He moved and pointed: 'You sir, will be implicated.'

She turned to look, the crowd murmured as they saw him pointing at the Governor.

'You will *all* be implicated!'

The audience laughed, they knew the traditions of May Day.

The story concerned a wicked king, played by Charlatan in a mask, who locked up his daughter in a tower because she loved a Grinder - Ren recognised Bark, wearing a half mask, flexing his muscles and grinning. Lilac gave a little gasp of recognition, then laughed quietly.

The resemblance of the king to the Governor was not lost on the audience, and the young boy who played the daughter wore a lavender dress. With plenty of villainy and buffoonery, the crowd booed and cheered. The Governor scowled and Ren heard him complaining to Count Saffron who replied:

'It's good for them to laugh at us once a year, my Lord. It's tradition.'

The peasants revolted and forced the king to change places with the Grinder. Everyone laughed at the king's inability to lift the Grinder's pestle. With the princess freed and her lover the Grinder crowned, they cheered long and loud.

When the cast sang the Grinder's song, many joined in:

'Our tools are fine, new and handy;

we carry them, to a man.

They're good for grinding, see them work!

If you want to feel them you can.'

A bunch of drunk young men in the crowd continued to sing the Grinder's song with gusto, adding lewd postures; Ren could feel the crowd's excitement. The Governor cried:

'This isn't tradition, this is debauchery! Grist?'

Grist came forward, the Governor spoke a few words. Grist nodded and motioned to some Barrow Guards. She saw them swoop like eagles through the crowd towards the knot of people who were singing loudly. Grist jumped up onto the stage, forcing the performance to an abrupt end. The audience cried out their disappointment. At the foot of the stage the Guards were forcing the singers apart. In a second it turned into a brawl - fists were flying, men were falling and rolling on the ground, women were pulling children away, people were booing. The fighting escalated as more Guards joined in: the excitement had turned to anger, and the mood spread like a cliff fire. The Guards were laying about young men with clubs, knocking them down, bloodying their heads and dragging them away.

Ren started forward; Lilac put out a hand to stop her.

The cast took a scrambled curtain call, bowing and waving. People protested as a bunch of young men were roped together and marched off by Barrow Guards. Charlatan called for peace. A sort of calm restored, the crowd drifted away in twos and threes, back to town, some still singing the Grinder's song. Charlatan stood beside the cart shaking hands and chatting with members of the audience. Ren looked for Bark, but he'd disappeared. Grist summoned Charlatan to meet the Governor; Count Saffron and Master Greenweed stood close by. Charlatan gave a slight bow, the Governor stood stiff and formal:

'We have enjoyed peaceful relations with Braymer.' He lowered his voice: 'We do not want foolish or wanton acts to cause complaint.'

'I will not be making a complaint.' Charlatan smiled.

'I'm not having a troupe of hobbledehoy actors upsetting the good order of the Isles.'

'Surely that is the tradition of the May Day Revels - to upset the order of things?' Charlatan smiled. Saffron nodded in agreement, and Greenweed added:

'It is important for the Gild - they work hard all year. Like a pot that boils, you need to let out the steam now and again.'

'Not at my expense! They undermine my authority.'

'Not at all, Sire. They confirm it.' Greenweed smiled.

'Governor?' Count Saffron urged him away, to his waiting sedan chair.

The Governor grew pale. Shrugging off Count Saffron, he turned back to Charlatan:

'My men are keeping close watch on you. Don't think that diplomacy will prevent me catching rats.'

He hooked his arm through Lilac's and urged: 'Come along, my dear,' marching off, pulling Lilac with him. As she looked back over her shoulder, Charlatan said:

'The lightest leaf floats best.'

Ren drifted through the crowd looking for Bark.

Lost in thought, she was surprised by a hand catching her elbow, an urgent voice:

'Ren!'

She came face to face with Vetch.

Chapter 2

Bark

He frowned and stared at her:

'What are you doing down here with us - the common folk?'

Ren stammered: 'An errand. . . for the Mistress of the Revels.'

He drew her to the side of the crowd.

'They've arrested a lot of Blue Hands. Some were beaten. It's not right.'

'You're safe?'

He leaned in closer and said in a low voice: 'No-one is safe from the Governor's bully men.'

Ren hesitated, 'I'd better go.'

'Just a minute, sister.' He grasped her tighter. 'Don't you care what happens to the Blue Hands now?' He took her hands and turned them in his own.

'You're one of them now.' He walked away, and Ren cried:

'How can you say that Vetch! Of course I care - I'm going to help them.'

Vetch turned. 'What?'

She stared at him, her words had slipped out. She backed into the crowd before he could ask more, his question ringing in her ears.

By flickering candlelight, Ren unknotted Lilac's laces:

'You told me the Mazards were going to help the Blue Hands. They didn't tonight.'

She searched Lilac's face, half in shadow. Lilac returned her look:

'What happened tonight shows the kind of ruler my father is. Island folk need to see it.'

'Blue Hands know how rules work.' She pulled at the laces of Lilac's bodice and skirt. 'There's nothing they can do.' She took the bodice.

'But maybe the Mazards can!' Lilac stepped out of her skirt, and paced, making the candle flicker. Ren clutched the clothes:

'What are you planning?'

'It needn't concern you.'

'You put me in danger!' insisted Ren.

'That's exactly why you shouldn't know.'

Ren folded the skirt and bodice, laying them in a chest.

'It would risk the safety of the group.' Lilac stretched and yawned.

Ren banged shut the chest:

'I've a right to know. So I can choose - .'

'You don't choose! You do as ordered.'

The words hit her like a slap on the cheek. She sat on the bed, trembling. Lilac put a hand on her shoulder:

'Mazards follow orders.'

'What about the Blue Hands arrested tonight?'

'Master Greenweed will deal with it.'

Ren stood up, shaking off Lilac's hands: 'But your father said..'

'The Blue Hands won't be charged. My father hates freedom and change. That's why the safe arrival of Azurro is important for our cause.'

Lilac walked away.

Ren persisted:

'Is he a spy - like Bark?'

'I'm tired, it's too late for explanations.'

'But..'

'No, Ren! You must learn. Discretion and Silence are vital for a Mazard as well as a maid.'

Visions of Bark kept her awake that night. She tossed and turned in her box bed, unsettled by the new direction her life had taken. She'd longed for excitement and imagined life beyond the confines of the dank Dyeing Sheds - Greenweed had picked her out, saying she was clever, special. What had she imagined? Elegant dresses, a stimulating and cultured life with an educated lady, perhaps a gallant young man to court her. Foolish thoughts, perhaps. But secret messages, spying? And Bark flustered her - she couldn't stop thinking of his skin, his hands, his voice, so much more vital and disturbing than the young men she knew. She forced herself to lie still and turned her mind to calmer thoughts of home, remembering that chilly February morning a few short months ago.

She'd had few possessions to bring with her as she packed to come up to the Hall, nothing important or valuable, except to her. The piece of serpentine, polished smooth over months by her mother so the red and green threads shone out like jewels. It was for her 13th name day: green for her maidenhood and red for her Flowers. Her Flowers hadn't come then, 'They will, soon enough,' her mother reassured her. A small pot of forget-me-nots, to remind her of home, and last of all, the Spelling Book that Greenweed had given her. The only book in the house. Precious because of that, but far more valuable for the gift of reading it had given her. It was the skill that led her here today.

As head of the Gild, Master Greenweed said he was looking for a Blue Hand to be taken on as a Lady's Maid. He thought Ren was just right.

It opened her up like an empty room being put to use.

She took particular care with her dress the next morning, knowing she would see Bark aboard The Starfish. She brushed her hair many times even though it would be hidden under her coif. As Ren followed Lilac down through town to the harbour, she watched her and decided Lilac's black hair and striking looks could carry off those Shebble shell colours only nobles were permitted to wear - blue, violet and black - the most costly to produce. However, Ren knew that the maid's colour pink suited her brown hair and hazel eyes. She smiled, thinking about Bark. Her curiosity wouldn't be contained:

'My Lady, where did you meet Bark?'

'In Braymer last year.'

'What's Braymer like?'

Lilac looked around: 'We're used to the salty tang of the sea. There, you can get so far away from the coast, that you're surrounded by earth. Even the houses smell of mud,' she laughed.

Ren made a face:

'Is that where Bark's from?'

'No more questions. Go on ahead and check that all's well. Just to be careful.' Lilac hung back, busying herself at a haberdasher's stall.

Ren was alert with all her nerve endings: her skin sensed the warmth of the sun, the touch of breeze, the roughness of sacking bales of wool and cotton. She heard the cry of seagulls, the Shebble Boats clinking in the harbour, men shouting, pulling ropes and winching hoists - but her eyes were looking for Bark.

She walked, her stomach tight in anticipation.

She saw The Starfish: a three-masted ship, decked with colourful flags. Then she glimpsed Bark with the actors, struggling to get their cart horse up the gangplank; the horse wouldn't move. She hung back behind the small crowd that had gathered, all throwing in words of advice on how to deal with animals on ships. He was dressed as a sailor in coarse bleached cotton. She noticed his fluid gestures, his ease with physical tasks as he stroked the horse to quieten it. He took off his neckerchief and tied it round the horse's eyes. The actors led it on board. She tapped him on the back, and as he swung round, his fierce look melted into a smile when he recognised Ren. They regarded each other a moment, then Bark looked away:

'Where's Lilac?'

With a flicker of annoyance, Ren turned and beckoned to Lilac. They climbed the gangplank and went down below. She watched Lilac and Bark clasp hands, saying nothing. Bark perched on the edge of a chest covered in a silken cloth. Lilac addressed them like a meeting:

'The Mazards have done well. And so has our newest member - Ren!'

Ren bit her lip, pleased despite herself, and gazed at Bark, willing him to look. When he turned his face to her, she smiled.

'An inspired idea to travel with the actors.' Lilac spoke to Bark. 'You have hidden skills as a performer.' She gave a small laugh.

'So you're not an actor, or a Grinder?' Ren puzzled.

Bark gave her a dazzling smile. Ren's stomach somersaulted.

'Now. Where is this treasure?' Lilac looked around.

Bark whisked off the large square of silk he'd been sitting on and revealed the chest. Made of sea-washed planks, the lid was nailed down and two straps with sturdy buckles were fastened round it. Ren watched as Bark undid the buckles and pulled the straps free. He took a forcer from his belt and worked its spike between the lid and the side.

With an effort he levered upwards; with a crack the top came off, revealing a layer of straw, sending dust into the dim light. Bark lifted it off. Underneath, the box was crammed with plants: long stalks with leaves and shrivelled wormy roots.

'Is that Azurro?' She bent over the chest, smelling earthiness and dry grass.

'It is.' Bark smiled.

All that secrecy for this, Ren thought.

Bark spoke quietly, 'These are worth all the Islands put

together.'

Ren looked at him, puzzled.

At a shout from above, they all started and Bark grasped the forcer tight.

'Good Morrow!' Charlatan's face grinned round the door: 'Well met, fellow Mazards.'

He swept in and spied the box. 'Aha, so is this what all the skulduggery's for!' He leant over, examining the contents.

'Master Charlatan, we are most grateful for your help in this matter.' Lilac shook his hand.

He bowed and then tapped his nose: 'As you know, some on Braymer will be interested in the outcome of your little enterprise.'

Ren looked round them all, wondering. Bark reached inside the box and drew out a small leather-bound Chapbook. Lilac took it and turned a few pages. Ren peered over her shoulder and noted pictures and diagrams, but instead of words, she saw a strange slanting pattern:

'Is it a secret code?'

Charlatan chuckled and Bark smiled.

'Yes and no,' he said.

'This book describes how to use Azurro,' Lilac informed her. 'A foreign script.'

'Can you read it, my Lady?'

'Bark can.' Lilac smiled at him. Ren stared at Bark, at this new piece of information that didn't seem to explain any more about him, but deepened his mystery. She looked back at the Chapbook:

'So what's Azurro for?'

Lilac snapped: 'What did I say about questions?'

'Why not tell her?' Bark urged. 'I think she deserves some explanations.'

Lilac folded her arms:

'What I'm going to tell you mustn't leave this room. Do you understand?'

Ren nodded.

'Azurro is a dye.'

Ren's eyes widened, her mouth dropped:

'.. a new dye? That's forbidden - the Charter is clear.'

Lilac nodded: 'That's why we act secretly. And why you must keep silent.'

'It carries the death penalty!' Ren burst out.

'That doesn't mean it's right.' Bark replied.

'The Charter protects the workers,' Ren said, dismayed.

Lilac blazed: 'People shouldn't be punished for trying new ideas.'

'Progress is worth taking risks for.' Bark agreed.

Ren retreated into a corner. She'd thought the Mazards was a nobles' game that Lilac played: a secret society, spies, hidden messages. Now a cold fear crept round her.

'Any word from the Alchemist?' Bark looked over at Lilac.

'He'll contact. When it's safe.' Lilac replied.

'How long?'

Lilac shrugged. She turned to Charlatan:

'My father was unsettled by the play yesterday. As Mistress of the Revels, I apologise for the heavy-handedness of his men.'

Charlatan roared with laughter:

'What is theatre for, if not to stir the emotions? When the audience response is lively, we know we've done our job well.'

Ren watched them laughing but remembered the workers beaten on the Dancing Fields by Guards. What did these Mazards know or care about the Blue Hands? And now Lilac was using her against the Gild. She thought about leaving, but where, who could she turn to, cut adrift from her roots and duty-bound to her Lady?

Bark came and sat beside her.

'The Mazards have good intentions.'

Ren hung her head and said nothing.

'You'll understand one day.' He leaned closer and whispered: 'We're not wicked, whatever you imagine.'

She looked into his eyes, trying to read them.

'We can trust you, can't we?'

Held by his gaze, she couldn't form words.

Charlatan bade farewell and Bark began filling a sailor's canvas sack with the Azurro from the chest.

'I need another place to stay.'

Lilac frowned: 'Somewhere out of the way.'

'The less I'm seen, the better. I didn't like the look of the Governor's man.'

'Grist is ruthless, he has no regard for law,' Lilac agreed.

Ren gasped at Lilac's hypocrisy. Bark didn't seem to notice. Lilac turned to Ren:

'You know the back streets - can you think of somewhere quiet?'

Bark pulled the neck of the sack tight. Ren put her hand to her throat, and blurted out:

'What about my room?'

Lilac scoffed: 'Ridiculous idea - right under Grist's nose!'

'Perhaps that's the last place he'd expect?' Bark smiled, 'I can lie low.'

'What about Ren? Obviously she can't use the room too.'

'Why not?' Bark winked at Ren and she suppressed a laugh.

'No, no!'

'I could sleep in your room, my Lady?' Ren suggested.

'What?'

'You have a bed, Lilac. Surely there's room for two?' Bark cajoled Lilac, who reddened:

'Will it be safe?'

Ren nodded, then realised Lilac was looking at Bark. He said:

'We'll walk together. As if I'm carrying goods for you.'

Lilac sighed, 'We must realise what we are committing ourselves to. This is a long journey. Once begun, there's no going back.'

Ren's eyes widened, expecting more surprises.

'The journey of life, our little company, working together. Who knows where it ends?' The planks beneath their feet rocked gently. Outside the cabin, a seabird cried. Lilac spread her hands.

'We must swear an oath.' She took Bark's hand and Ren's. Bark grasped her other hand, completing the small circle.

'A solemn vow of silence. One protects all, all protect one.'

In turn Lilac and Bark repeated 'I vow.'

Ren hesitated. Bark gave her hand a squeeze. She looked at him: 'I vow.'

Lilac urged Ren to climb onto deck first. She looked all around, relieved to see sailors and warehouse men, the normal hustle and bustle of the quayside.

Bark, head down, the canvas bag slung over his shoulder, fell into step behind Lilac. Ren kept looking round, but saw no-one suspicious. Free from the spell of Bark's eyes, she trembled. What had made her offer her room and commit herself to more danger? She glanced sideways at Lilac:

'My Lady..'

'Sshh.'

Lilac walked, stiff and pale, her eyes fixed ahead. Ren peered at every corner and shadow, imagining dangers, breathing as if she couldn't get enough air. She reflected on the Mazards; they lied, they did foolish, dangerous things when they didn't need to. She considered the dangers Blue Hands faced every day, without choice, simply to earn a living. Like Moss - the day of her accident was still vivid. The dank shed was loud with crackling fire, the hissing of hot dye, terrifying and exciting. The Mistress had told Moss to pour in the fix - a pot of piss. She leant over too far. In a flash, boiling liquid leapt up and spat at her young skin. Her screams filled the thick air. The Mistress had to pull her hands from her face to throw cold water. Too late, her cheek and chin were badly burnt. Women were often speckled with blue marks - the Shebble Pox they called it. Moss's case was bad. She was ill for weeks. Her skin healed with blue pocks, but the scar inside was tender; Moss couldn't talk of it without flinching.

That was why Ren's mother thought she'd be safer up at the Barrow Hall. Now Ren saw there were other unimagined dangers that could surround her, confusing and trapping.

As they neared the Barrow Hall, they agreed Lilac would enter by the main door and Bark would follow Ren through the kitchen. If anyone asked, Bark was carrying new banners specially ordered by the Mistress of the Revels. The cook and kitchen staff stopped to stare briefly as they walked in, then returned to their work.

Once inside her room with Bark, Ren stood in silence, aware how small the space was, certain her heart beat too loudly as they waited for the knock that signalled Lilac at the door. It had been easy, too easy, Ren feared. Bark took the Chapbook and one plant out of the sack and looked around:

'We must hide the rest.'

Clumsy with nerves, Ren opened the drawer beneath her box bed and stowed the canvas sack inside, beneath her clothes. Bark kept the Chapbook and gave the plant to Ren. He pointed out features, although Ren hardly heard, watching his fingers, their heads close together, trembling at the danger she held in her hand. At the three short knocks, they turned to see Lilac walk in.

'Perhaps this will do.' She said looking about. 'Three short raps will be our signal. Ren can bring you food and messages.'

Ren was about to protest when the door flew open. She froze as Grist appeared:

'Caught like rats in a trap!'

Chapter 3
Caught

Two Guards squeezed in behind Grist, one thick-set and weather-beaten, the younger one pink and nervous. Grist stood there regarding them all, pleased with his catch. Bark looked up at the window.

Grist grinned: 'There's nowhere to go.'

Lilac demanded: 'By what right do you enter here?'

He laughed.

'Sir?' The young Guard had taken the plant from Ren and showed it to him.

He folded his arms and growled:

'What's this?'

Ren looked from Lilac to Bark, neither of them spoke.

'Article 5 of the Gild Regulations.' Grist frowned at them. 'Importing foreign plants is a serious offence. Tie him up. And her Ladyship.'

The younger Guard took hold of Lilac's arm, who protested: 'You have no reason to apprehend me.'

Grist ignored her and examined the plant.

Bark twisted away from the older Guard, trying to hide the Chapbook. The Guard found it and held it out.

Grist waved it triumphantly.

'Information about the tides.' Lilac told him. Grist looked at the lettering and illustrations:

'Don't take me for a fool.' He pocketed the book.

Bark struggled, protesting.

With quiet menace, Grist said: 'I'll give you something real to squawk about soon.' He turned to Lilac.

'I've been watching you for some time. I'm sure your father will be most interested in your *revelry.*' Grist jabbed a finger: 'I have a pretty fair idea of your habits, and acquaintances.'

Grist looked Ren up and down. 'What about you, girl?'

Ren blanched and her legs turned to water, her mouth dry.

'She's my new maid,' Lilac replied.

Grist raised an eyebrow and grunted: 'Search the room.'

Ren watched the young Guard look around on top of the canopy of her bed, then lift the covers; her heart nearly stopped when he opened the drawer beneath her bed. He reached down, saw her chemise and hose, blushed scarlet, and closed the drawer.

'Nothing here, sir.'

She breathed in relief but her thoughts were racing - spying, breaking Gild rules, importing illegal plants - the Governor will show no mercy.

'Listen my Lady,' Grist's voice became conspiratorial. 'What if I just forget that I ever saw you. Then I might come to you now and again for a little information?'

'No.'

'Your father need never know.'

Lilac tossed her head: 'Say what you like to my father. I make no deals with people like you.'

Grist growled: 'House arrest for my Lady. Lock-up for him'

Ren and Lilac exchanged a quick glance, leaving Ren none the wiser as the older Guard led Lilac away, pushing her up the stairs.

She followed Grist and the younger Guard as they marched Bark back down through the kitchen. The staff stopped working and watched them pass. The doorkeeper stared when the band arrived at the East Gate. Shadows were lengthening as Grist and the Guard escorted Bark up the alley, away from the Barrow Hall. She watched them disappear, wanting to say something to Bark, but what? She was at a loss, she had no orders, everyone ignored her. Nothing Lady Rose had taught her could have prepared her for this confusion.

Her mother's voice came into her head: *You can't think on an empty stomach.* Tired, Ren pushed through the maids and servants discussing the turn of events and went into the kitchens. The staff fell silent as she entered. The cook sniggered:

'Ah, it's the Blue Hand - come for some broth for the prisoner?'

In her few months at the Hall no-one had ever called her that before. How quickly attitudes could change. She took a breath:

'Two bowls,' she replied, ignoring glances as she carried the food up to Lilac's quarters. The Guard outside the door opened it for her and she went in:

'M'Lady?' she called to Lilac, who was staring out of the window.

'Ren, is that food? Just what I need.'

Lilac smiled but her lips were trembling. Ren ate her broth in silence, though burning with worry and questions. Lilac sighed:

'At least they do not have the rest of the Azurro. Grist is a fool.'

Ren glanced towards the door:

'Keep your voice down m'Lady. The Guard may be listening.'

'Yes, of course.' She whispered: 'You'll have to be my eyes and ears now.'

Ren said nothing, but her heart sank as she picked up the bowls. They were nearly knocked out of her hands as the Governor burst into the room. He stood there, hands on hips, eyes dark. The Guard hovered, Ren edged back to the wall.

'My Lord,' the Guard began. The Governor waved his hand:

'Wait outside!'

The Guard gave a slight bow and closed the door. Ren watched Lilac closely.

'Oh father -' she gave a little choking pause, 'there's been a terrible misunderstanding.'

'What's going on?'

'I wanted to talk to one of the actors about trade with Braymer.'

'Why? Actors are fools and worse.'

'So I can help you, father, and be useful.'

The Governor frowned: 'We have Ministers and Officers to do it. Procedure. A right way and a wrong way, Lilac. You don't know which is which.'

Lilac flushed.

'Stay out of trouble. That's useful. I made you Mistress of the Revels. Isn't that enough?'

Lilac grew pinker: 'Father, of course I'm interested in plays and dancing. But -'

'Girls do not involve themselves in trade or politics.'

Lilac's face fell, Ren could see her struggle to keep the tone light: 'You are so old- fashioned.'

'And you are a liar. What's this plant Grist found? You've been planning something.'

Ren stifled a gasp.

Lilac blanched: 'No.'

'Do you realise how serious your meddling is?'

'I'm not meddling. You don't understand -'

'By the Southern Rose!' The Governor roared, grasping her arm. 'Don't dare tell me what I don't understand!' He pulled her close, twisting her wrist.

'Ow!'

The Governor glared and let her go. Lilac rubbed her skin. He sighed.

'Life seems easy to you. Let me tell you what I understand: peace, stability, trade - they have to be maintained by hard work and vigilance. Rules have a purpose. You cannot flout them on a whim.' He went to the door.

'Father, please! Don't leave me locked up.'

The Governor contemplated her request:

'A few days to think about your fate will help you come to your senses.' He lowered his voice. 'Don't interfere. I determine the way Calico is governed.'

Lilac clenched her fists.

'My men are watching,' he warned and his eyes flicked over to Ren before he strode out.

Lilac fell back onto the bed and began to sob. Ren watched her for a moment, then mumbled: 'I'll take the bowls,' rushed out of the door and bumped straight into Lady Rose.

'Running, Ren?' Rose blocked her way, 'What is the urgency?'

Ren said nothing, staring at the ground. Rose sighed and walked on. Leaving the bowls, Ren hurried to catch her arm.

'Lady Rose, may I talk to you?'

Rose glared at her, then commanded: 'Come.'

They climbed a flight of stairs to a part of the Hall Ren had never seen before, to a long corridor that echoed. There were no carpets or tapestries adorning the walls. Lady Rose walked at a determined pace until she reached a door halfway along. She looked up and down, opened it and pushed Ren in. It was a room much like Ren's but bigger with a window onto the back lanes.

'Sit.'

Looking around at the walls and the furnishings: two pots of herbs, a few books and a frame of half-finished embroidery, it was clear this was Rose's personal room. To her surprise, Rose stretched up for a bottle from a shelf and set two dainty glasses on a table and poured an amber liquid into both. She handed one to Ren, who hesitated to take it.

'It's not poison!' Lady Rose sipped. 'Calico mead.' She look at Ren expectantly:

'Well?'

Ren fiddled with a strand of hair slipping from her coif.

'Not even a week and you are...' Lady Rose waved her glass and closed her eyes. 'I worked hard to teach you, did I not? You looked the part, you - oh.'

Opening her eyes, she fixed them on Ren, and said:

'The skills of a maid have been practised for hundreds of years. Yet you disdain them.'

'Lady Lilac has no liking for rules. She said you, I mean they, were old-fashioned.'

Lady Rose flushed:

'When they asked me to train a Blue Hand as a Lady's maid, I had two thoughts. First I said - No. Impossible. Second, I thought why?' She sipped again and said nothing more.

Ren held her glass tight:

'Lady Lilac asks me - to do things that you never taught me.'

Rose paled and her mouth opened as if to speak. She seemed to think better of it and as she took a sip of her mead, her hand shook a little. She kept her eyes on Ren.

Ren pushed on: 'She treats me as if I'm her equal. But I'm not! And, and.. '

'Be careful what you say.' Rose said quietly.

'She makes me carry secret messages.'

Lady Rose said nothing.

Ren gulped her drink, and blurted out: 'I want to go home.'

'You may visit, with agreement from the Hall. Though now Lady Lilac is..' Rose rubbed her temple, 'who knows what the protocol is.'

'I mean leave the Hall. Stop being a Lady's maid.'

'Ren..'

'Find someone else to serve Lilac! I'm a Dyer.' Ren cried and jumped up, flushed with frustration.

Rose got up: 'Remember what I said.' She pressed firmly on Ren's shoulders. Ren closed her eyes and counted to ten, her breathing slowed and her shoulders relaxed. Rose went to look out of her window, saying nothing for a while, staring out at the evening sky. Then she sighed and turned back to Ren:

'There was a formal agreement, you're indentured for three years service.'

'Three years?!'

'The fortunes of the nobles are not ours to question or defy.'

'You said always obey. Always?'

Lady Rose massaged her temples a moment, she looked tired.

'Patience and discretion are the most valuable skills at a maid's disposal.' She spoke more gently: 'Lady Lilac needs you more than ever, now she's confined to her room. We who serve have our duty.'

She went and opened the door. Their conversation was at an end.

Back in her room Ren tore off her coif and threw it down:

'Stupid thing!'

The mead had gone to her head. Dizzy, she clasped herself, trying to imagine her mother's arms around her. Footsteps outside on the stairs made her stop and hold her breath. She waited a moment, went to the door, opened it a crack and looked out. No-one. She shut it again and knelt at her bed, opening the drawer. She slid her hand in, under her clothes, feeling for the rough canvas sack. It was still there. She breathed, closed the drawer and sat staring at the window as the sky grew dark.

* * *

The next morning she woke with a start, dreaming of a man in her room. Pulling the curtains of her bed, her eyes rested on the blue forget-me-nots in their pot, and a painful longing for home settled on her. What should she do? She feared staying in her room and worried about leaving it. She had to speak to Lilac.

She brought a tray of food to Lilac's room and found her lying on her bed. She put the tray on the table. Lilac didn't stir.

'M'Lady? Your breakfast.'

Lilac said nothing, then Ren whispered:

'The Azurro.'

'I can't think - I have an ache in my head.'

'What if they come searching?'

'Just leave me.'

'But..'

'Go.'

Lilac said nothing more, so Ren left, biting her tongue.

She crept away and climbed the stairs to the Turret that she'd first climbed with Lilac. The only place she thought no-one would find her. She sat and cried. The tears helped, and she became calmer.

It was the highest point on the Barrow Hall. They never kept a Watch here nowadays. Her grandfather was the last who remembered any threat to the Isles during the Dye Wars. He said the harbour bells would ring out a warning many times a year. Ren couldn't remember when the bells had ever been rung in these days of peace since the signing of the Charter. Maybe that would all change with the Mazards.

Lilac had said Go. But where? She breathed the salty air blowing off the sea from the south, and looked over the immense blue of the Silk Straits to the other Islands: Shebblebed, Fairholm and Herd. Behind her were the moors, purple with heather, rising to Mount Sisal, a rocky outcrop covered in snow all Winter, which melted and filled the town wells in Spring. Her eyes searched west, a coast of coves and wild cliffs, to The Dancing Fields where she'd met Bark at the play. Where was he now? Ren thought about everything that had happened in just a few days. Like Charlatan's play, it seemed as if everyone acted a part. All except her, with no idea how to behave. Was she a maid, a conspirator, or simply a Blue Hand out of her depth?

She turned east to the Allotments on the edge of the city, busy with folk and pictured her mother there, feeding her chooks, picking herbs for the evening broth for Vetch. Her mother, always calm, full of simple wisdom. She'd promised to visit - could she talk to Vetch? He was angry with her.

He might be even angrier when he found out what she'd got involved with. She daren't tell him.

She looked down to the market, the long Dyeing and Drying Sheds, and thought about her last day there and Greenweed escorting her up to the Hall. He was Master of the Gild, surely he could allow her to return to the Dye Sheds? She smoothed the creases from her skirts and stepped down into the stairwell with a purpose.

Outside her room, she put an ear to the door and listened. Turning the handle gently, she let the door swing open. The room was empty. She knelt again at the drawer under her box bed, and sighed as her fingers touched rough canvas. She pulled out her cloak and set off, telling the Gate keeper she was on an errand for her Mistress.

Along the sea walls were big stone buildings; some were warehouses, others, merchant houses, but one was the headquarters of the Gild. It was imposing, with many storeys and steps up to a carved door. A blue banner flew from the roof. The parapet displayed gargoyles, grotesque faces carved in stone: cruel-eyed devils or pouting fish that spewed when it rained, carrying water from the roof tops. Some were set in walls at shoulder height, hooded men's faces or lions, all with enormous mouths that could take a roll of parchment. These were letter boxes for the great houses and businesses. She kept to the shadowy side of the street. The stone was cool and rough. All was quiet as she climbed the steps, and lifted the metal hand knocker. A loud clang echoed through the street.

After a while the door was opened by an old man in green breeches and jerkin. His eyes were cloudy and he shaded them with ink-stained fingers:

'Good Morrow.'

'Sir, I have some business to discuss with Master Greenweed.'

'Is he expecting you? He said nothing to me.'

'No - I came hoping..' She trailed off.

'Oh? Well, come in. We don't get many young ladies visiting.' He gave a dry whispery laugh and shut the door behind her. They were in a gloomy lobby with tiled floor and murals of the Shebble trade on the walls.

'Have a seat, lass.' He indicated a wooden settle and shuffled away.

The air had a whiff of chemicalles and dust. She sat, tapping her foot, then stood again and looked more closely at the murals. One depicted Shebblers, men perched on ledges at the base of steep cliffs, hauling up nets of shells; another showed men in the Grinding Shed, pouring sacks of shells into the basin where a great grinding stone rolled round and round. At the Dyeing Shed scene - light and airy, full of pretty, clean young women - Ren laughed out loud.

'Not very realistic, I admit.'

'Master Greenweed.' She smiled.

'Welcome, my dear.' As he spoke he guided her into a room off the lobby, dominated by a long table surrounded by chairs. He sat next to her, with a kind, concerned expression.

'Now. Has your Lady sent you?'

'No. No...'

'I have heard some - rumours?' He raised an eyebrow.

Ren cleared her throat, clasped and unclasped her hands: 'What have you heard?'

'That Lady Lilac was apprehended, with another, smuggling an illegal plant?'

Ren nodded, 'My Lady is confined to her room.'

'And this other person?'

'Taken to the Lock-up I think.'

Greenweed rubbed his chin, then stood up, 'I'm forgetting my manners. Would you like some refreshment?'

'A cup of water, if I may.'

He went to the door and called: 'Fettle! Water please!' He turned to Ren, smiled briefly: 'He's slow, but reliable. Now why did you pay this visit?' He watched her face.

'I.. want to leave Barrow Hall. Be a Dyer again.'

'I see. Have you discussed this with Lady Lilac?'

Ren shook her head:

'There are plenty of other maids.'

'She was most particular in her wishes. I chose you carefully.'

'But.. I didn't - it isn't what I expected. All this..' Ren stopped, afraid to say too much.

Greenweed nodded and took her hand: 'However, you are indentured for three years.'

'Can't you do something, as Gild Master?'

A knock interrupted the conversation and Fettle shuffled in with a tray with two cups and a jug. They stayed silent as he poured and offered Ren a cup. Greenweed shook his head, and Fettle left the room.

'Rules are rules.' He spread his hands, and looked regretful.

She drained her water, and stood, pulling her cloak around her, mumbling thanks, her heart sinking. Before he opened the front door for her, Greenweed asked quietly:

'And where are these illegal plants now?'

She stared at him. He came closer.

'Did your Lady hide them?'

She lowered her eyes.

'You can trust me.'

She stepped back and shook her head.

'I, no… There was only one plant.'

'Really?'

'They only found one.' And she scurried down the steps before Greenweed could ask any more questions.

Chapter 4
Home

'Food, my Lady.' Ren set the midday meal of greens and cheese down and was about to leave when Lilac called:

'Wait!' She came close and whispered: 'I want you to find out how Bark is.'

'How am I to do it?' Ren's voice rose in resentment. 'And what about the..' Ren lowered her voice, 'bag, in my room?'

'Keep it safe. Speak to no-one about it.'

Ren pulled the door to behind her.

Back in her room, she turned over possibilities in her mind. Perhaps she should go to the Lock-up. She had to admit she wanted to reassure herself that Bark was alive. Now was the moment to wear a disguise - as her true self. No-one would question a Blue Hand going about town. She pulled out her old homespun dress and brown cloak. It itched and smelt of wood fire. She took off her coif and plaited her long hair. She'd be quick, and get back before the evening meal. She left by the North gate, and turned towards the Barrow Court Lock-up. She walked along alleys and paths where the street cats, ginger and tabby, were sunning themselves like sleepy door stops.

Dressed as a Blue Hand again she felt more like her old self and yet like an imposter too. With her white hands, she looked like the girls in the mural at the Gild headquarters.

Now, she wanted to hide her hands. She walked through the alleys aware that the Dyers would be hard at work with no freedom to wander in the fresh air. Her thoughts came to an abrupt halt as a young man blocked her path.

'Hello Ren.'

She gazed, confused for a moment by the sun in her eyes.

'It's me, Kale.'

'Kale?'

He worked with Vetch in the Grinding Shed and was declared the most handsome by Ren's friends. They'd been considered a good match. Her pulse raced a little quicker.

'How are you liking it up at the Hall?'

'Oh, you know - music, balls, banquets and young courtiers.' She rolled her eyes.

Kale took her hand in concern.

'Do they bother you? You should take care. We worried about you. Some of the lads. Well, me.'

Ren smiled at him.

'It's not funny. Those nobles think they have rights over their servants, to use them…'

Her smile faded, she took his arm and they walked together.

'I'm all right. I can look after myself.'

'I know!' Kale laughed.

Ren laughed too: 'How are you? Not at work?'

He looked away. 'Bit of a cough. Been to the Spittal.'

'Oh.' Ren knew that meant Blue Lung. She hugged his arm, not knowing what to say.

'Where are you going then?' Kale asked.

'A secret errand for my Mistress.' She winked, trying to make light of it. 'Tell no-one you saw me.'

'I won't.' He hesitated then kissed her. 'Sorry. Had to do it one last time.'

They stopped and stood facing each other, holding hands across an invisible divide.

'Take care.'

'And you, Ren.'

They turned and went their separate ways.

From a short distance, she watched the Lock-up for a moment - a one-storey square building with barred windows and two heavy wooden gates, wide enough for a cart or carriage. Taking a breath, she entered through a small door set in the left gate and smiled at the Guard:

'I bring a message.'

The Guard didn't smile back, but stood aside to allow her to pass through. She stepped over the door frame and found herself in a courtyard. To her right, through an open door, she glimpsed a table with papers and books. Her knees shook as she walked straight in and stood before the clerk at the table. She nearly lost her nerve when she saw the Chapbook lying on his desk.

'Yes?' he said without looking up.

'I wish to see Captain Pallet.'

The man, his sage green doublet unbuttoned at the neck, regarded her briefly, then bent to his writing:

'He's out. On business. Should be back in an hour.'

She stood, uncertain what to do. The clerk indicated a

wooden bench. Ren sat and made herself melt into stillness. For the first few minutes she heard the scratching of his quill on parchment. Then a Barrow Guard stuck his head through the door and hissed:

'He's coming, look sharp.'

The clerk seemed nervous, even afraid, as Grist sloped in and stood with his back to her, barely three feet away. Ren drew her hood up and sank back onto the bench. The clerk spoke in low tones:

'Did he confess?'

Grist wiped his brow, then pulled on his jerkin: 'No, pretty boy's tougher than he looks. Strappado, thumbscrews. No use.'

Ren clasped her hands to stop them trembling. The clerk picked up the Chapbook on his desk:

'What about this? I couldn't make head nor tail of it.'

Grist grunted: 'Must be foreign. This is an Article 5.'

The clerk nodded.

'What now?'

'I wish I could get my hands on that barefaced Lilac. She knows a thing or two.' He balled a fist and slammed it on the table. The clerk jumped. Ren saw panic cross his face.

Grist growled: 'She's safe in her room, damn it,' and pocketed the Chapbook.

The clerk coughed:

'What shall we tell The Harbourmaster?'

'I'll speak to him.' Grist shook his head: 'When he finds out some plant has slipped in under his nose!'

'What about the other theatricals from Braymer?' The

clerk hesitated.

'They sailed before we could search the ship, curse it.' Grist paused: 'Lilac's maid is bound to know something. I'll pay her another visit.'

Ren held her breath.

The clerk nodded. 'What shall we do with the prisoner?'

'Throw him in the 'gettory. Wet his heels for a bit, see how he likes that. And if he says anything - come and tell me, no-one else. Understood?' Grist swung round and walked out straight past her. She breathed, fighting the urge to run, and made herself sit still a while longer. When the clerk was deep in his writing again, she left.

Running back, keeping an eye out for Grist or Barrow Guards, she knew he'd be coming for her sooner rather than later. She had to get rid of the sack of Azurro. In a blind panic, all she could think of was to get it out of her room. If only she could reach the Hall before Grist. As she slipped into the back entrance to the kitchen, the evening meal was being prepared: pans sizzled, cauldrons steamed and lots of hands were chopping and peeling. Cook called out:

'Hi. You're late.'

'No, I'm Lilac's maid…'

'Don't look like it to me. Not in pink, is she?' He looked around for affirmation.

The other kitchen staff sniggered.

'Anyhow, the Lady's shut up in her room. And I'm short handed. Get peeling those potatoes.' He indicated a large tub of brown mud.

'But..'

Red-necked and towering over her with a large knife, he said:

'I'm not having any buts from my staff. Here!' He pointed to a bowl and knife. 'Jump to it.'

She looked round. She could see no-one was on her side.

'A Hall full of folk don't get fed by magic.' The Cook grumbled as he went back to his meat joint. She saw him wink at someone - he knew who she was all right.

Biting her lip, she took off her cloak and rolled it up under the bench and started to peel. She kept looking up at the door, scanning the room, expecting Grist any moment. She worked in a hurry, missing bits of peel. When she brought the bowl to the Cook he glanced and grunted:

'Call them peeled? I want them done properly.'

She gripped the bowl tight and went back to her bench. She spent another ten minutes checking through all the potatoes, cursing herself at taking longer than if she'd been more careful in the first place. This time she was humble before the Cook.

'I've finished. I really must see to my Lady, if I may be excused now?'

He kept chopping meat into smaller pieces as if he hadn't heard. She waited, holding her breath. She saw the faintest of nods. Grabbing her cloak she flew up the stairs, laughter following her.

She halted outside her room, waiting for her pounding heart to still. She stood for a long moment and put her fingertips on the wood, as if they could sense what was inside. Listening hard, holding her breath, she pushed the door open. All seemed calm, her room looked untouched. Ren changed into her pink dress, pinned her coif over her plait and hurried up to Lilac's room.

The Guard outside glanced at her and nodded. She knocked and entered. Lilac was reading. She looked up and whispered:

'Any news?'

'I went to the Lock-up.'

Lilac nodded.

'Grist was there. He was this close! I just sat quiet. Didn't recognise me in my old clothes.'

'And Bark?'

'He was there. Grist said he didn't talk.'

Lilac paled and put a hand to her mouth. 'He's been tortured!?'

Could that be her fate at Grist's hands too? Ren pushed the thought away, 'Grist was very angry - said something about the 'gettory?'

'The 'gettory... Oh Bark.'

'It means he's alive. Doesn't it?' Ren searched for reassurance.

'For the moment.' Lilac replied.

'My Lady, the Az -'

'I must think of a way to help him.'

'My Lady, Grist said -'

'I'm starving. Is that part of my punishment?'

'But..'

Lilac raised her eyebrows.

Ren flushed. 'I'll go straight away.'

Holding her herself tall, she entered the kitchen. No-one made any remark at her transformation to maid, but she felt eyes on her and heard muttering as she walked away with a tray of coney stew and a plate of strawberries. Let them talk. Gossip was easy to bear compared to what Grist might do. All Lilac thought about was Bark. What about Ren's own danger? She would insist, after the evening meal, that Lilac do something to help her. Surely Lilac could think of another hiding place for the Azurro, or even just confess and hand it over. She didn't care, as long as she didn't have to be involved. She couldn't sleep in that room another night. She longed to go home.

As Lilac sat eating, Ren took her chance.

'My Lady, I heard Grist say he would question me. What if he searches my room? Finds the - you know. I don't want it. I can't sleep, I'm too afraid.' All her worry and anger boiled over. 'I didn't ask for this!'

Lilac looked at her as if seeing her anew.

'I want to go home. Lady Rose said I'm entitled - ' she grew less bold, 'with your agreement.'

Lilac laid down her bowl and spoon.

'You are a Mazard and swore an oath. You suggested your own room yourself!'

Ren hung her head. Lilac was right.

'I didn't know what I was agreeing to. I - please let me go home.'

Lilac bit into a large strawberry and considered.

'No. I need you here. Eyes and Ears, Ren. I'm blind without you.'

'Just for a day.'

'No, no I can't do without you.'

Ren slumped and ate a strawberry, tasting nothing.

She sat up:

'I could take the Azurro, get it away from the Hall?'

Lilac thought a while: 'Yes. Perhaps. If we can get it to your home..'

'My home?' Ren had imagined hiding it in a shed or even throwing it off a cliff.

'No-one will look there. Yes. Go later tonight, after dark. When it's quiet.'

They agreed that Ren would leave once the Hall staff had finished in the kitchen, and she'd dress in her old clothes again. When she worried what to say if asked about the sack, Lilac made no suggestion, other than to say:

'Surely Blue Hands carry *bundles* all the time? No-one will think it unusual.'

Ren considered that for all Lady Lilac's education, she was ignorant about ordinary life. It hit her like a knock on the head - of course! That's why she wanted her as a maid. Lilac had said it, but Ren only fully understood the significance now. She needed Ren's knowledge. Mazard, was just another fancy name for servant.

She lifted the sack. It was heavy and awkward to hold under her cloak. Ren tiptoed down the stairs to the kitchen.

Bathed in a red glow, it was warm from the cooking embers. No-one was around. Lifting the latch, cooler air surrounded her. She swung her bundle over her shoulder and, hugging the walls, went round to the east gate.

She lowered the sack again, under her cloak:

'Visiting my mother.'

The Gatekeeper let her through: 'Bit late to be out. Better take care.'

Although bent under the canvas sack, Ren stepped lightly as she headed for the allotments and home. The stars lit the sky like diamond dust. She breathed the salty air and smiled at how surprised her mother would be to see her. She thought of Moss, wondering whether she missed her. Ren had asked to stay friends, but what effort had she made to keep in touch? Ren was in a different world to the Dyers and Blue Hands. If she knew, what would Moss think of her actions? Shifting the pack to her other shoulder, she kept to the back streets. She'd never been out on her own this late, and had to be careful. Despite its familiar smells of sea air spiced with roast fish, she knew the town was different at night, especially down by the harbour. The mood was more feral and predatory.

Men were looking for women, who laughed and waited in the shadows, or stood under lanterns hanging in doorways. There might be cutpurses, interested in her sack. Burdened with it, she couldn't walk as fast as she wanted to. A tall man called:

'Hello Missy, need a strong man to carry that for you?'

She kept her head down, ignoring him. Down a narrow alley her heart sank as she saw a group of men, lounging, leaning against a wall outside a rough drinking den. There was no way round, so she kept on. Seeing her, they pushed off the wall and stood grinning, forming a barrier. When she drew near they whistled and jostled her:

'Hello honeypot.' She attempted to push past - a hand grabbed her skirt: 'What's the hurry?' A rough hand pulled at the sack: 'What have we here?'

Fear of discovery made her fierce, she pulled away and faced them, shouting:

'Leave me be!'

'All right - no need to bite!'

'Only being friendly.'

'I like 'em frisky!'

The men laughed as one followed her: 'Aw, give us a kiss, just one. Go on.' She ignored him, until he too gave up and went back to lounging with the others.

Round a corner, hidden in the shade of a giant fig tree hanging over a wall, she dropped the sack and eased her shoulders, her sense of freedom dissipated. How could she arrive with the Azurro, what explanation could she give? She shouldn't be bringing danger to her family. She turned arguments over and over: hide it, throw it away, explain it all to Vetch and ask for his help? Then he'd be implicated; this was serious. Swinging the sack up onto her shoulders again, she questioned her loyalty to Lilac. Vetch was a Gildsman. The Charter was the law. His livelihood was at stake. What was Lilac risking? Her father was Governor!

Her pace got slower as she grew nearer home but no closer to a solution. Why had she said she'd take the wretched

Azurro? She sighed - at least it wasn't under her bed.

Entering into the allotment gate she wandered in the starlit dark down rows of sprouting leaves and flowering fruit bushes, washed by soft green scents. She recognised her mother's plot, full of herbs and vegetables and dropped her burden by the chook house, a wooden hut on stilts to prevent rats getting in, closed up for the night with a door pegged shut to keep out foxes. She squatted and took the peg from its slot, and looked into the black interior. Half a dozen sleepy chooks shifted and settled on their perch. It would have to do. She pushed in the canvas sack, squashing it under the perch, in amongst feathers and droppings. The birds squawked and fluttered at the intrusion.

'Sshh.' She put a hand out, a hen pecked her. 'That's right. Guard it for me.'

She replaced the peg, stood up, brushing her skirt and turned down the next row, heading for home.

She could make out a pot of marigolds and nasturtiums by the front door. The sight raised her spirits. She stopped. How small home was.

She opened the door and stood on the threshold.

Vetch and her mother sat at the table, staring in silence. Her mother came to her, held her face, kissed her brow and ran her hands over her shoulders, picking off a feather, saying nothing about the old dress and cloak.

'Tis good to have you home.'

'Ren?' Vetch stared at her: 'What's this?' He pulled at the skirt. 'What're you doing here?'

'Have you eaten?' Her mother asked. 'What about a hot

drink?'

She tore mint leaves from a bunch in a pot, dividing them between three mugs. Vetch eyed Ren:

'So? What do you know of these rumours?'

Her mother took a pan off the fire, holding the handle with the edge of her skirt, and poured water into the mugs:

'What rumours?'

'Spies, two arrested!'

Ren looked from Vetch to her mother, wondering how news travelled so quickly. She opened her mouth, then closed it and took her mug of mint tea. Handing Vetch his mug, she wouldn't meet his eye.

'You must have heard something,' Vetch pressed her.

Her mother frowned at Vetch. 'Sh. Let her be,' and sipped her tea.

Now she was here, Ren didn't know how to talk to her family, or what to say.

She stared into her mug:

'Do you ever wish that I had stayed a Dye girl and kept at home, mother?'

'Do you?' Fern replied.

Ren looked up: 'Yes... I don't know. I've learnt new skills...'

Vetch snorted. 'A little bit of sewing and fiddling with ribbons. Easy.'

'No - it's Lilac - my Lady's not what I expected.'

Her mother leaned towards her:

'Does she treat you unkind?'

Ren shook her head, struggling to explain: 'She's more like

a, a bossy sister.'

'You're *not* her sister..' Vetch scoffed at the idea.

'I know! She said she chose me -'

Vetch eyes widened: 'Because you were a Blue Hand?'

Ren nodded.

Fern was puzzled: 'Does she want to learn to dye?'

Ren snapped: 'No.'

'What *do* you do for her then?' Vetch demanded.

She was treading a fine line. She wanted to ask Vetch's advice, yet the more she told, the more she'd endanger him. And she'd taken an oath to The Mazards.

'So?'

'I - you know, errands. I don't fiddle with ribbons!'

'Ah,' said Vetch, 'is this what you meant at the Dancing Fields, about helping the Blue Hands? Did they let them all go?'

'Let who go?' Ren asked, thinking of Bark. 'No, he's not a Gildsman.'

'Who's not?'

'Oh, I - .'

'So you *do* know about the spies who've been arrested.' Vetch looked triumphant.

Ren shook her head, then nodded, she was getting tied up in knots. She sipped her tea and tried to think.

'What's this all about?' Fern asked. 'Explain it to me.'

Vetch and Fern waited expectantly.

Ren took a big breath: 'Lady Lilac said - what if there was a new dye.'

Chapter 5
The Prophecy

Vetch stared at her: 'What?'

'A dye that was easier to make.'

Vetch smacked his hand off his forehead: 'Are you a fool? This is the only place in the cosmos for Shebble shells.'

'I know, but..'

'That's what gives our dye value!'

'What's this to do with the Lady Lilac?' Her mother frowned.

'Don't be taken in by clever talk, Ren.' Vetch wagged a finger.

'I'm not.' Even as she said it, she wondered if it was true.

'Those nobles have velvet tongues but sharp teeth,' Vetch warned.

'Just because your hands are white, don't think that makes you one of them,' her mother said and looked down at her own hands, rough and worn.

'I know! I'm just telling you what she said. That people are prevented from trying new ideas.'

Vetch threw his arms in the air in disbelief.

'Why have you been talking about this?' Fern asked.

Ren hesitated, confused. She covered her face with her hands, protecting herself from the barrage of questions. Vetch grasped her face and stared into her eyes. She tore her eyes away.

'Ha! So now we see whose side you're on.' Vetch strode around the little room. 'It's just as I said. Now you work at the Barrow Hall, we don't matter to you.' He glared at her. 'You've turned your back on your own family! You see with the eyes of the Barrow Hall.'

'Maybe I see things you can't.'

'What do you mean?' He pounced on her words. 'Tell me, sister.'

Ren could have bitten her tongue. Vetch folded his arms, looking stern. She wanted understanding and support, not these critical expressions. She peeped through her fingers from Vetch to her mother, at her sad eyes:

'Ren, what have you got mixed up in?'

Her mother's gentle question made Ren burst out crying. Her mother gave her a handkerchief. Vetch brought her mint tea, and rubbed her back.

When her heaving sobs calmed she drank some tea, wiped her eyes and began to talk. Vetch and her mother listened in silence, exchanging glances now and then.

Vetch whistled.

'So Lilac is one of the spies they were talking of in the Sheds today? The Governor's own daughter!' He thought for a while, then looked up: 'And you've seen this plant?'

'Yes. There's a whole bag of them. Hidden.' She blushed. 'And the Governor's man is looking for me!' She sobbed again.

'You're safe here,' Fern soothed.

'But what will the Mazards do with the plants?' asked Vetch.

'They talked about an Alchemist.' Ren looked at him.

He returned her look. 'That can only mean one thing.'

She breathed: 'They're going to make a new dye!'

He pulled his ear: 'I know all the dye makers on Calico. They'd never break their oath.'

His mother shook her head: 'Men may do all manner of things for reasons you know nothing of.'

'It must be a foreigner.'

Ren sobbed: 'I wish I'd never gone to the Hall!'

'You need to find out more. We must bring this to a meeting of the Gild.'

Ren shook her head. 'I don't want to go back. No. I can't.' She sat with her head in her hands.

Her mother said: 'Everything will be clearer after a good night's sleep.'

Before Vetch left for work the next morning, she begged him to keep quiet about all she'd told him.

'Yes. Of course.'

She hugged him in relief, glad he was being kinder and more understanding.

'I won't say a thing until you bring more evidence.'

She ate a bowl of porridge with her mother. Although it was early in the morning, the sun was already burning through a misty white haze. Her mother kissed her.

'I'm off to water my greens - we're set for a hot spell.' She stood a moment longer: 'Take care.'

The purpose of her visit achieved, she had no choice but to return to the Hall and retraced her steps with reluctance.

She'd hidden the Azurro. But now she fretted whether it would have been better to have told Vetch and her mother about it. Perhaps her mother might find it. Ren was certain she'd keep quiet, and what then? If Grist attempted to force secrets from Ren, how brave would she be? At least she alone was responsible, not her family. She took an erratic course through town, avoiding chance encounters, thinking every man might be a spy coming for her.

She was hot and itchy in her old brown dress and her jaw ached from her clenched teeth. She tried to sing one of her old Blue Hand songs as she walked - it was hopeless. Lilac wanted her to be her eyes and ears. Now Vetch expected information. She was under pressure from all sides. But who was looking out for *her* safety and needs?

Nothing was amiss in her room, and she changed back into her maid's outfit and collected breakfast.

'Ren! Was your visit home..useful?'

'Yes, thank you my Lady.'

With Lilac confined to her room, Ren's duties were reduced to bringing food and books from the library. She avoided Lilac's searching eyes and determined she would give her as little information as possible. As she cleared breakfast dishes, Lilac asked for another book that morning,

'The Charts of the Cosmos. A book of maps.'

She found the book; it was huge and awkward to carry. She had a struggle bringing it back. Despite herself she was curious and lingered beside Lilac, running her fingertips over some raised lettering on the leather binding, covered in gold leaf that glinted in sun light.

'What are these my Lady?'

'Maps show what shape a country is, where its mountains and rivers, cities and roads lie. It can also show what manner of things are to be found in the countries. This collection also shows all the seas, and islands, planets and stars, great and small. It's very precious.'

Lilac turned the pages carefully. Ren could see intricate line drawings of shapes and signs, of names and numbers. She had never seen such complex and rich images. Hardly daring to breathe over it, her eyes took it all in like dry earth absorbing rain.

'Who made all these?'

'Many people, from all over the world. It's ancient.'

Lilac opened a particular page and pointed. Ren pored over it, examining every detail:

'The Calico Isles? Yes. There's Shebblebed, all long and thin! And Calico, look, that's the harbour with tiny boats in it.' Ren breathed: 'It's beautiful.'

They both stared, not speaking as Lilac turned the pages.

'There are so many maps. The cosmos is so big,' exclaimed Ren.

'It's important to know these countries and who rules them, whether they're friend or enemy.'

'To be prepared if they attack?'

'Or whether we might trade with them.'

Lilac turned to a page of one big circular map. 'This is a map of the whole globe. All of it.' Ren leaned close to see strange animals with huge ears and tails for a nose, women with claws and wings, fish rising out of the water as big as houses. The world was larger and full of more possibilities than she'd ever imagined. Lilac pointed to a spot near the centre of the circle: four tiny dots hardly visible.

'There are the Isles of Calico.'

'So small?'

Slowly Lilac moved her finger so Ren could follow it, round the Isles, up along the coasts of bigger islands. Her finger stopped at a large country near the top of the map.

'That is the land of the Braymer. They live between mountains, with sea all round. Seafaring folk, the same as us. And great traders.'

'Where the wool comes from - the land that smells of mud,' Ren whispered.

'Yes. And here,' Lilac's finger drew across an ocean to a land mass in the south east, 'is Samara.'

Ren repeated the word under her breath, 'Samara', liking the sound of it.

'All of that is Samara. That's where Azurro is grown.'

Ren gasped. It could have fitted Calico in many hundred times over.

She stood up: 'Will that be all?'

'Yes.' Lilac waved a hand as she sat at her table to study.

Back in her room, Ren opened her narrow window and stared at the sky, as blue as a bolt of cloth dyed on Calico, thinking about the maps of the cosmos. Samara was beyond her imagination, that one country could be so large! She saw, too, how small her own knowledge was compared to Lilac's and wondered whether she might be allowed to read any of the books in the library as Lilac did. Books gave up their information freely. You could trust books. She would educate herself.

Ren knew if she kept out of sight of Lady Rose, who demanded details of her errands whenever they met, she could find time for her own pursuits and, as she still hadn't encountered Grist, she began to relax a little.

At the southern quarter of the Hall, on two tall doors were the words Barrow Hall Library - Silence. She pushed in and stood listening: a fly buzzed in a corner, high windows let in golden rays of light. She was alone. The room was divided by blocks of shelving that reached from floor to ceiling. Books were held in place with iron filigree work and the topmost levels were reached by a pyramid of steps, set on a base with wheels. The Library had a pleasant scent: dry paper and sweet cedar wood. The smell of knowledge, Ren decided. Where on earth should she begin? The books were arranged in subjects and by letter, mainly about the Calico Isles. She walked along the shelves noting Alchemy, Buildings, Creatures - Dyes. She pulled one out.

'A Hundred Years of Dyeing on Calico', fat and heavy, full of dates and numbers. She put it back, running her fingers along the brown leather spines: The Alchemicalle Process of Shebble Dye; Dye Trading Laws; Dyeing and Weaving on the Calico Isles. A red volume caught her eye: The Travels of a Calico Captain in Samara. It had a miniature map of the cosmos on the first page.

She laid it on a long table, mouthing the unfamiliar words.

She read how this sailor had reached and mapped the coastline of Samara and dwelt in the country for years. He described crossing great plains, many days' walk, that had no cities or buildings on them, but occasional bands of folk would pass by, herding animals unknown on Calico. He traversed chains of high mountains that reached up to the sky, at the feet of which were fertile valleys that grew fruit and plants in unimaginable variety and abundance. The country had many Warlords, rulers who maintained order in their provinces, all in the name of the supreme Overlord of Samara.

The descriptions of palaces, wild animals, customs and rituals fascinated her. The Captain admitted his surprise that, for all their rulers' power and wealth, these people had little in the way of skills and machinery to manufacture goods, and particularly cloth, on a large scale. It was all laboriously hand-made, in a much more simple fashion than on Calico. He expressed the opinion that anyone who might broker terms of trade with this mighty people would benefit from cheap, abundant raw material, particularly Azurro.

Ren's pulse quickened as she read the words - he described it as a plant growing in profusion, like a weed, yet it made a most enduring dye that, in the Captain's opinion, rivalled Shebble in depth and subtlety of its hues. With a tingle at the roots of her hair Ren read the passage again.

'Azurro is a *blue* dye!' She cried.

The Captain prophesied that Samara could surpass the Calico Isles in the supremacy of cloth and dyeing, if they learnt to harness their own natural resources. She sat back, her thoughts racing - Samara was a giant country compared to the tiny Calico Isles. If they could make a blue dye more easily and in greater quantities, Calico would lose its one great advantage in the world of trade. Did Lilac want to wreck the Shebble dye industry?

Yes! That explained the Mazards and their aims - Azurro would *replace* the Shebble shell, destroying the whole business of dyeing on the Calico Isles! With a lurch, it dawned on Ren that the prophecy was coming true and she'd been helping to bring it about. A pit opened up in her stomach - What had she done? She put the book back on the shelf. Boiling with anger, she paced up and down, fighting the urge to run straight to Vetch with the shattering news.

'Calm yourself,' she said aloud, 'Think.'

She had to act with care, and not attract suspicion. It was midday, she still had her duties. She left the library, her thoughts whirling and went down to the kitchen to collect platters of shellfish and samphire.

As soon as she entered the room, Lilac held up a letter, but said nothing, mouthing the words *for Bark*, Ren nodded to show she understood.

'Your food, my Lady,' she said. She banged the plates down and took the letter, stuffing it into her pocket. It smelled strongly of vanilla. She said nothing during their short meal, afraid she couldn't control her tongue. As she cleared away the plates, Lilac whispered:

'You will get it to him, won't you?'

'I don't know, my Lady.'

'Oh, you'll find a way.'

Angry and agitated, Ren left without another word; she

had to clear her head and think.

She crept up to the Lookout again, to keep out of sight. The sun was hot, the air still. The sea mirrored the sky and all the buildings in town shimmered in heat haze. She lent on the parapet, turning matters over in her mind, cursing herself for being too trusting and helping the wrong people. It was the Blue Hands who needed to know the terrible truth about the Mazards and Azurro, and it was down to her to tell them.

Out of nowhere a hand came round her mouth and another round her waist, pinning her arms. Struggling, unable to steady herself, she was forced forward, swaying above the town.

'Quiet,' a voice hissed. 'It's a long way down.'

Ren stopped struggling, the arms around her relaxed and she put a hand out to steady herself. Turning, she came face to face with Grist. She scrambled away from him.

'What you doing up here? Shirking no doubt. Oh, I know your type. Pretty as a lark, but cunning as a cat.' He chucked her under the chin. She turned her face away, putting a hand on her pocket, aware of Lilac's letter. Her heart beat too fast, her breathing shallow. He turned her cheek to face him.

'Conspiracy to import illegal plants? Serious charges.'

She licked her dry lips, and looked down over the edge.

'Lady Lilac's locked in her room. Pretty boy won't talk. But you can.'

'If I don't get more information, I'll have to force Bark's tongue to loosen.'

Her head jerked up.

'Like pretty boy, do you?' Grist laughed.

'Where is he?'

'The Forgettory. Dark as night and the only way out is up, into the Lock-up.'

He watched her, letting his words sink in.

'So why don't you help me, and help yourself?'

She shook her head.

Grist drew level with her, his tone reasoning: 'You come from Blue Hands don't you? They respect the Charter. But those two! They play act and cause a stir like fools.' His eyes were locked on hers. 'They don't care about the ordinary folk. The likes of you. Young, hardworking. Attractive.' He put out a hand and stroked her cheek.

Ren pulled away, breaking free of his fingers, looking out to sea. He pressed behind her. She could feel his body, his breath on her neck. His arm brushed hers as he pointed to the Dye Sheds:

'Think of all your friends in the Gild.'

She stared down into the streets, busy with workers, unaware of this scene high above them.

He moved his hips as he said: 'Got a special boy have you?'

He had her pinned to the parapet. She squeezed out from his grasp and went to the other side of the tower.

'He'll suffer if Lilac has her way.'

'She wants to help them.'

He gave her a pitying smile, and shook his head.

Ren opened her mouth to speak, then shut it again. She turned her back to him and gazed up at Mount Sisal.

He coaxed: 'Listen. My grandfather was a sailor, lost his

life in the Dye Wars. See, we're on the same side.' He crossed over the tower and leaned in to her ear: 'If you helped me, you'd be helping your own folk.'

Ren longed to confide her terrible discovery about Azurro and Samara to someone.

'Your Lady and her friends think they're above the law.'

'But they're not!'

'So why protect them?'

She looked into his smiling face, but saw his eyes cold and calculating.

'Your men were violent to the workers at the May Day Revels.'

His smile vanished: 'The Governor has his way of keeping order. I obey him. That's the Law.' He grabbed her face, squeezing her cheeks and twisting her head so that she saw the dizzying drop over the parapet. 'They're heading for a fall and they'll pull you with them.'

Ren's stomach lurched. He let her go. She put a hand to her cheek, staring, breathless.

Grist pointed a finger: 'I want names. Information. You'd be doing yourself a favour.'

He disappeared down the stairwell. Ren slumped for a long while, shivering despite the heat beating down on her head.

Chapter 6
The 'gettory

She must have been sitting there for half an hour or more, she wasn't sure. Her head thudded, her eyes were bothered by flashes of light. Everything she saw had double outlines. Desperate for liquid, her tongue swollen in her mouth, she didn't trust herself to stand. She crawled to the stairwell, nausea rising in her throat. She forced it back, making her way down into the coolness of the dark. She stumbled into the kitchen, asking for water. Cook looked at her with shrewd eyes and put a hand to her forehead:

'You have Sun Fever. Fool. Too much heat. Go and lie down.'

As she made her way, trying not to spill the water, Cook called after her:

'Sip it slowly, not big gulps or you'll vomit,' and chuckled.

Ren lay on her bed, head aching, slipping in and out of fevered sleep, aware of a beam of sunlight that moved round her room like a slow finger. Sometime later she started awake at a knock on her door:

'Who is it?' she called.

'Nutmeg. From the kitchen. Got a chamomile tea for you. Cook says it'll help.'

She fell back on her bed: 'Come in.'

A skinny kitchen girl entered, hair escaping from her scarf, her brown apron dark with oil spots. She held a steaming mug out to Ren.

'Thank you, Nutmeg.' She had no desire to sit up. 'What o'clock is it?'

'Near to sundown.'

'Is, has.. my Lady had her evening meal?'

The girl shrugged.

'Dunno,' and wandered round the room, touching Ren's things. 'It's all the talk in the kitchens; spying and such. Is m'Lady really a smuggler?'

She stood at the end of the bed, her eyes alight, waiting. Ren said nothing, Nutmeg twisted her fingers:

'Well, better get back then.'

The door closed with a thud.

She sipped tea and slowly her head cleared - she reflected on what she'd discovered about Samara, about Azurro, and remembered Grist's threats, on top of the tower.

Grist was right. She didn't want to help the Mazards: Lilac deserved her ill-fortune, it was nothing to do with Ren. She was a Blue Hand - and white skin didn't change that. She couldn't bear to stay another day at the Hall serving Lilac. She was caught, a slave, she had no power over her life or her being. Pushed and pulled from all sides - the Mazards, the Governor's man, her brother and the Gild. All wanting information, wanting her to spy and deceive. What did she care about indentures and documents? She wouldn't be at Lilac's beck and call anymore. She lay there, waiting for her legs to stop trembling.

She'd take her the last meal tonight and tell her just what she thought.

The Cook looked up at her as she entered the kitchen. 'Better?'

'Yes. Thanks for the chamomile.' She managed a smile. 'I'd better see to my Lady.'

'Here we are - pickled pork and greens. Don't eat too much if you still feel a bit -' he waved his hand - 'Y'know.'

She climbed wearily up the stairs to Lilac's corridor. The Guard let her in; Lilac was still reading at her table. Without looking up she snapped:

'What kept you?'

'Grist.'

Lilac sat up at the mention of his name.

'He tried to throw me from the tower.'

Lilac blanched, then smiled: 'Oh, he threatens, but he won't..'

Ren banged the plates down: 'You're the threat!'

'Shh. Keep your voice down.'

Ren took a breath, counted to ten and in a harsh whisper said:

'It's a *blue* dye...'

Lilac cut her off: 'A little knowledge is a dangerous thing, Ren.' She gripped her shoulders tight: 'I've offered you opportunities no other Blue Hand has ever had.'

Ren raised her arms, throwing off Lilac's hands in an angry gesture: 'I trained as a maid, to do maid's work. Not this...skulking. I won't do the Mazards' work.'

'It's too late.' Lilac shook her head.

'It's got nothing to do with me!'

Lilac whispered: 'Only you know where the Azurro is.'

Ren sat and stared down at her plate of food. 'At least as a Blue Hand I knew who I was!'

Her stomach churned, her head thumped. The room was hot and airless. She longed for everything to stop. Tomorrow, she vowed to herself, she'd go home, tell Vetch what she knew.

Outside, black clouds built up, darkening the sky. A flash of lightning lit the room. Lilac opened the window and sniffed the air.

'A May storm is coming.'

Coupled with snow melt, a heavy May rain could fill the Sisal river. Some years it broke its bank and parts of the town were feet under water. A terrible thought lodged in Ren's mind, rousing her from misery.

'My Lady. If the 'gettory is underground...?'

Lilac turned to Ren: 'It will flood. By the Southern Rose! '

'What can be done?'

Lilac sat, thinking.

Ren walked back and forth: 'Your father's the Governor. Surely he can do something?' She went to the window as another flash split the sky. She turned: 'What about the Mazards - won't they help?'

Lilac shook her head:

'It would endanger everything. No.'

'But - he might drown!'

Lilac went to the window beside Ren: 'They won't let him. He's more valuable alive.'

Ren tossed in hot sleep, thunderclaps woke her, flashes of

lightning lit the night.

A grey dawn found her sleep-deprived and confused. Heavy rain was falling. Bark dominated her thoughts. She imagined a dark underground chamber slowly filling with water and no escape. As she dressed, her hand found Lilac's letter, forgotten in her pocket. She threw her cloak on in disgust: she wasn't Lilac's go-between, Bark wasn't her responsibility. She would go home, before the roads were mired and anyone could stop her - get rid of the Azurro once and for all. She hurried down the stairs, out through the kitchen door and ran to the east gate. The Gatekeeper was drinking a mug of tea and keeping dry.

Pulling her hood up, she ran through a world of grey rods, yet as she hurried along alleys she found her feet carrying her towards the Lock-up, not home. If the Mazards weren't able to save Bark, well, she had to try.

A few market folk were dashing from doorways, holding baskets or sacks over their heads. She blinked and ran blindly. Hair escaped from her cap, plastering itself to her forehead - she wiped it aside. The muddy lanes caused her to slither and slide, her dress hung heavy, clinging to her legs. She didn't look about to see whether she was being followed. She had only one thought in her mind.

She tried to remember what little she knew about the 'gettory: reached by a trap door in the floor of the Lock-up. Perhaps the 'gettory was *meant* to flood and drown forgotten prisoners. Knowing the river ran under his prison seemed her only clue - there must be a way the water got in.

Ren stumbled on through the lanes, awash with rain pouring off roofs and out of gutters, slewing plant pots from side to side. She dodged the rubbish and tumbled chairs until, round a corner, she saw the building, grim in the downpour. She hurried straight past the Lock-up, heading for the streets behind, hunting for the course of the river and where it might drop out of sight underground.

Beyond another street of stables and workshops, the land opened out, to a raised grassy bank, and further off, a wooden bridge - the river must flow beneath that, she thought. Her feet slid on the wet grass, but once over the top of the bank she saw the racing river, heard its throaty roar and, looking down away to the left, saw it enter a stone culvert. She gauged where the Lock-up might be and guessed the culvert must run directly under the building. She slithered down the bank onto a narrow footpath beside the river, steadying herself, and headed forwards. Would it be a dead end or would it take her closer to Bark? The pathway carried on into the culvert and she stared into the mouth of a tunnel waiting to swallow her.

Could she, should she step inside?

She hesitated, fearful of the dark terrain, but also of what she might find: Bark, disfigured and broken. She wouldn't think of that. Her heart hammering, desire to prove herself drove her on, a test of body and will.

The tunnel enclosed her. It stank of the middens, noisy with racing water. The side wall was slippery under her palm as she balanced on the ledge, one person wide, aware of the power of water, black and swift on her right, that could sweep her away under the curved roof if she slipped. She edged forward, stooping to avoid the weed dripping from above, fingering her skin. The light gleamed dully on an iron gate shut across the path, with barbs on the water side. In frustration she rattled the rusty lock; it snapped and the gate swung wide in a dangerous invitation. Now she had two choices: turn round or commit herself to the unknown. She pictured his face, imagined him calling and no-one coming.

Splashing through water lapping over the walkway, her leather shoes sodden, the torrent deafening as she peered into the gloom, her fingertips traced the slime as she edged forward. As it grew darker, she had to force herself on, sensing the tunnel around her. Her palm detected a change, the stone wall ended. She touched wood, a strip of metal. She ran both hands over the surface, searching the metal with her fingers, found hinges, bolts and a small grating at eye level, dark as a starless night inside. She called: 'Hello?' her voice overwhelmed by noisy water. She called louder through the grating:

'Bark?' and again: 'Hello?'

Fingers reached through the grating, feeling for hers.

'I'm here,' she cried, fumbling with hands awkward from wet and cold, trying to pull bolts. They wouldn't move. Frantic, she took a deep breath and tried again, working each bolt back and forth, up and down, to ease its stiffness before she tried again to slide it free. She pulled hard and wrenched the first one open, then the second, finally a third, smashing her knuckles each time. She licked at the red wounds. Water dragged round her ankles as she pushed the door inwards;

it scraped, groaning, resisting. Out of the darkness came a hand; she grasped it and he stumbled into her.

'It's Ren.' Could he see her, understand? 'The tunnel's filling.'

'My arm...' he clung to her, wincing in pain.

She faltered under his weight. He reeked of stale sweat. She balanced on the narrow ledge, turning around:

'Follow me.' Ren reached out for the slippery wall with her right hand to steady herself, aware of Bark clutching her shoulder behind her. 'This way.'

The torrent dragged at their legs, roaring and gurgling, swallowing the rainwater pouring through the storm drains emptying out the town. It threw tree branches before it, carried smashed fences; reckless, it rose around them. They inched forward against the barrage up to their thighs. Her foot slipped and Bark lost balance. They struggled to keep upright. A faint light filtered in ahead.

'Look out!' she cried and flattened herself to the wall as a mad barrel boomed into the entrance, missing them by inches. Neither spoke but fought forwards. They passed the metal gate, and kept fighting towards the grey light, until they reached the entrance and clawed up the muddy bank, sodden, smeared with rust and slime, panting. Ren threw herself down at the top of the cut, her heart banging in her chest. Bark fell down beside her, groaning and lay there, spent.

After a while, he sat up, grimacing in pain. His eyes had dark circles round them. His filthy clothes stuck to him:

'I must put this right.'

She could see his left shoulder all misshapen. She paled.

'Take my hand. When I say, pull.'

She shivered, shaking her head.

'It must be done.'

He took her hand and made her grasp his limp one, watching her face. He winced, then:

'Now!'

She pulled.

'Ah!' he cried.

He bent his elbow, flexed his fist and nodded.

She could see his arm sat right now.

He looked up into her face with a passion Ren had never seen there before. He kissed her cold hands.

'You came.' He fell back again, eyes closed. 'Thank you.'

Forgetting the rain, the muddy bank, she knelt staring at him lying there, unguarded in exhaustion, and had an overwhelming desire to kiss him.

'Take off your jacket,' she said, undoing his buttons, gingerly slipping his jacket sleeve off. He held his arm across his chest and she re-buttoned it, trapping his left arm inside the jacket in a makeshift sling. His eyes met hers.

'Where's safe?'

What did he mean? Ren could think of nothing but the feel of his lips on her hands.

'I need somewhere to stay. What about your home?'

'No!' She thought of the Azurro, already a threat to her family. If Bark hid there too, it would be disastrous!

She tried to focus; the last few days were all mixed up in her mind. Suddenly words came into her head:

'The Mazards - ' She looked at Bark. The rain tumbled down.

'What?'

'What are you planning?' she demanded. A crack of lightning lit up the sky.

'We must get away!' he urged.

She leant forward: 'Grist threatened to cast me from the Hall Tower!'

'What did you tell him?'

'Nothing.'

'The Azurro?'

She sat with her head in her hands:

'It's hidden..'

'Good. Now, I must hide.'

He crawled up the bank and took a swift look over the top. He turned and winced as he shifted his arm, closing his eyes. Ren watched him then she stood up and began to walk away. His groan stopped her, she turned back. He looked broken; she noticed his skin had a sallow sheen. Despite her misgivings, she sighed:

'I know a place, west along the cliffs.'

She bent and helped him stand; they scrambled up and over the bank and down the other side. She looked around at the landscape, grey and blurred, and set off. Bark stumbled after, grim, as rain ran down his face. She couldn't stop shivering. Her hair hung from under her cap in wet strands, sticking to her neck. Clenching her teeth to stop them chattering, she rubbed her hands to bring warmth and movement back. Bark walked wrapped in silence.

They crossed fields, and gorse-covered moors. Their drenched clothes clung to them. They avoided farmhouses, and at one point crept across a bridge over a swollen stream, meeting no-one.

Ren focused on finding a path, cutting west towards the cliffs, the long grasses whispering against their legs.

'Where is this place?' he asked.

'Husher Cove. You can reach it by boat or coast path. There's an old adit in the cliff face.'

'Do many people know it?' Bark watched her.

'The mine's abandoned. Blue Hands go there sometimes.'

'You're from Blue Hands?' Bark raised an eyebrow, and smiled for the first time.

'Is that good?' She smiled back.

The silence between them melted. The rain eased, the dark clouds grew ragged and she took sideways glances at his unshaven face, imagining what the feel of his skin would be like. When his arm brushed hers, it burned.

About midday they arrived at a deserted stretch of coast. A low sky rested on sea the colour of tin. Set in cliffs dotted with pink thrift and green succulents, they climbed down a cleft with crude steps cut into the rock, worn smooth by feet over the years. It led to a rocky inlet, a tiny harbour, enough for a couple of boats. Half way down she turned onto a ledge overhung with grasses and feathery tamarisk. She walked along, looking, then she called:

'Yes, here it is,' and disappeared through a curtain of green. Ren stood at the entrance to a hidden tunnel leading into the side of the cliff. It dripped with spring water at the mouth, but inside was dry and large enough to take a man, stooping. They peered in.

'How far?' Bark's voice echoed in the tunnel.

'A good few yards, it's blocked by an old rock fall.'

Bark slumped down at the entrance.

'I haven't slept or eaten or washed. I don't know what day it is.' He sighed.

Ren bent to him:

'You should get out of your wet clothes, let them dry.' She helped him remove his jacket. He winced as his left arm came out, then he sat cradling it against his brown chest.

'And now you.' He smiled up at her.

She took off her cap, her hair plastered flat to her head, aware of his eyes as she removed her outer skirt, mud-spattered and dark with water, but kept her chemise shift on. She laid the clothes on the grass.

'Samphire grows hereabouts. There'll be Sea Beet too.' Ren suggested: 'You can drink the water dripping from the cliff, it runs from a spring above.' She went foraging, and left Bark sitting. She gathered the bright green plants that sprouted between the rocks, and brought handfuls back. She caught his scent again: sharp and foreign like a wild animal.

He reached out a hand and she sat beside him.

'Thank you.'

She gave him spiky samphire and beet leaves.

He tore into it and between mouthfuls eyed her:

'You're fearless. A seabird, made for adventure.'

A thousand ways of starting a sentence came to her, but she couldn't seem to open her mouth. She was both angry and drawn towards him, wanting to ask questions, demand explanations, but she simply sat and watched him. She collected water in a clam shell, refilling it a few times to slake his thirst.

He yawned. She said: 'You need to sleep, rest your arm.'

Ren gathered long grasses from the cliff top and made a makeshift bed inside the rock tunnel:

'You'll be hidden in here.'

Bark lay down and closed his eyes. Ren stood watching, then stretched out beside him. She took his good arm and wrapped it round her shoulder, he held her tight to his chest. They lay close and shivered. As they warmed up, she drifted into sleep.

Chapter 7
The Gild

She woke and sat up close to the still-sleeping Bark, listening to sea and wind, watching a watery sun emerge from the clouds. She thought back to other times at Husher Cove; it was a place popular with young couples who couldn't find privacy in small crowded cottages. Many Blue Hand girls and lads had gone into marriage early because a baby was on the way. She'd been careful not to get tied down like that. She liked Kale, he was good looking, but he didn't excite her like Bark, who was unpredictable and strange. He was dangerous.

He woke and she looked at him, smiling.

'Good afternoon.'

He pulled her down: 'You saved me.' He leant in and brushed her mouth with his. Her lips buzzed.

'One last thing for me,' he whispered.

She closed her eyes, expecting more kisses: 'Yes?'

'Deliver a message. To the Alchemist.'

Her eyes flew open, a red flush rose up her neck, her ears burned.

'But I'm being watched by Grist. It's not fair.'

'That's the lot of a Mazard.'

'Oh, the Mazards? I didn't sign my name.'

Bark flashed her a dark look: 'You took a vow.'

Ren stood and cried: 'I'm told nothing, except to do as I'm told.'

'Perhaps it's safer.' He put out a hand to her. She ignored it and accused him:

'It's a blue dye, this Azurro. It'll ruin the dye trade!'

'Yes.'

Before she could speak, Bark added:

'And no. There's no simple answer.'

'I just want to know the truth.'

He rubbed his hand over his eyes: 'Listen.'

Ren sighed, and looked away.

'I'm going to tell you about a great People, whose land stretched from west ocean to east sea; a country so large it would fit your group of Islands many times over.' He patted the ground.

She sat beside him, with her back to the stones and watched his profile as he talked.

'It had places so hot, nothing would grow but hills of sand that would twist and change with the wind. There were high mountains, covered in snow all year round and long rivers that brought snow melt to water rich valleys.'

'What -?' Ren began. Bark raised a hand and carried on:

'There were many varieties of animal, good to eat and plants of great delicacy and power in cooking. They had mines that held gems and precious metals. These people built magnificent cities, and had a vast population.'

He glanced at her, to see if she listened. Ren nodded, thinking of the book The Calico Captain. He turned back to the view out of the entrance.

'There were wise men who could read the pattern of the stars and see the future. An ancient prophecy foretold that strangers would come across the water and steal a secret that would change their world forever. So, the King and his men of power sent out the order that all strangers stepping onto the shores of the country should be put to death, and never allowed to remain on their soil.'

'This is a child's story.' Ren folded her arms, listening despite herself.

'Then, one day, by chance a small foreign ship found the entrance to one of the wide rivers and sailed up right to the heart of a city. The chief of that place, a clever man, and curious, reasoned: "While the stranger is on his ship, he is not on our soil. Therefore what harm is there to talk, maybe visit his ship? Perhaps learn something." So began a dialogue: in signs at first, but the longer the ship remained, the more fluent the stranger grew in their language, and - '

'I don't understand why you're telling me this ancient tale,' she complained.

Bark turned and gave her a wry smile:

'Why do you think, Ren?'

She closed her mouth and look down at her hands. 'What happened in the end? Tell me the stolen Secret.'

'Knowledge. Once the stranger could communicate with the people, he'd broken through their barrier. It led to understanding and accord, trade and exchange.'

'But why was that a danger to the city and the King?'

Bark's face lit up. 'Exactly! Should a country protect itself with walls and rules, and live in isolation from the rest of the world, never changing? Or is it better to share knowledge and goods, increasing wealth and trade?'

'I think it sounds better to share knowledge.'

'So do the Mazards. We don't look back to the past. We imagine the future.'

Reluctant to leave, yet aware that she had a long walk ahead, she picked up her bag and cloak. Bark drew aside the foliage from the entrance, looked out, then back at her:

'Will you do this one last thing - deliver a message to say where I am? Lilac will tell you where to take it.'

At the mention of Lilac, she remembered the letter she was supposed to give to Bark.

She wouldn't give it to him.

Cross with herself for feeling jealous, and angry with Lilac too, she didn't want to remind him of Lilac's existence.

She claimed him with a kiss on the cheek: 'I'll try and do as you ask. Be careful with your arm.'

He held her and kissed her lips: 'Thank you again, fearless seabird.'

The heat rose in her neck. She smiled.

'I'll return with food, if I can. It may be days.'

'I'm used to waiting.'

Smiling as she walked, she relived every moment of her time with Bark - his parting kiss, tasting him, his salty foreignness. She laughed, glad that she'd kept Lilac's letter.

After walking half an hour, resting on a granite outcrop facing the wide Straits of Silk, aware of the letter in her pocket, curiosity drove her hands. Looking around to ensure she was alone, her fingers trembled a little as she broke the seal and smoothed out the parchment, arguing that she must read the letter if she was to discover the Mazards' plans. She began to read, the scent of vanilla clinging to her hands:

My Dearest,

if you are reading this then Ren has found a way to contact you in your dismal prison. I write to let you know that I too am a prisoner, confined to my rooms. I suffer no hardship as you do my dear, but no treacherous word shall I speak.

My will is strong – I know you are strong too, even though I fear they may use you cruelly. Be brave. As soon as may be I will find a way to release you, have no fear. If necessary, I will contact the Samarans for your father to intercede, though I know you wish that connection to be kept secret for the moment.

Please send word back with Ren, a sign that you are faring well, or simply your greetings – I will know they carry your unspoken love.

> *I long for the sound of your voice, the touch of your hand;*
> *I kiss this page in your absence, till we meet again and*
> *I may kiss your living lips,*
> *Ever, Lilac*

The words hit her like a blow to the chest. She couldn't breathe, she gasped for air. Her throat hurt as if she'd swallowed a stone. Dropping her head to her knees, she sat there blank and empty for a long time.

She shivered, pulling her cloak closer as the sun dipped towards the sea. Stiff with cold, she didn't know what to do. She re-read the letter through tear-filled eyes, imagining

Lilac in Bark's arms. Angry too, that Lilac offered to help free him, but it was her, Ren, who'd risked her life to save him! Lilac's words were hollow promises, she wouldn't trust her ever again. And Bark was from Samara! It explained all the mystery about him: his accent, his knowledge and support of Azurro. It changed everything. One more reason not to trust the Mazards. Only she knew where Bark was. And she wasn't going to tell anyone.

But what to do now?

She couldn't return to the Hall - how would she stop herself saying things she mustn't to Lilac? Fearful of Grist too, she couldn't go back there.

She shivered again, and stared out at the endless blue of the sea, wishing she could simply sink into it and drift away like a leaf, not thinking, not feeling, just floating.

If she could get to the Dye Sheds, maybe Moss would help her? She looked down at her clothes, crumpled and mud-smeared. With her cloak pulled around her, surely no-one would take her for a maid from the Barrow Hall. She had an idea.

The wild bilberries were beginning to ripen. Off the path, in a sheltered dell where bushes were already fruiting, she gathered a handful of the small inky berries; they were bitter and unripe, yet crushed in her hand they made a dark stain. She gathered more and crushed two palmfuls, then rubbed her hands together to spread the dye. The colour was patchy - it wouldn't fool Moss, but a Barrow Guard might be taken in.

Light-headed with hunger and tiredness, she forced herself

to keep alert and watchful in case men were out looking for her. However, no-one seemed to notice her amongst the folk returning after a day's work; she walked as fast as she dared through the market. Three Barrow Guards were up ahead, watching the crowds. If she changed route now, it might look obvious. Keep walking, she told herself. As she passed them, they burst out laughing and one man stepped back into her path. Shocked, she stopped.

'Mind yourself, clumsy,' one Guard berated the other, who turned to her:

'Where are you going?'

'Leave her; she's just a Blue Hand.'

He turned away, they laughed again. She walked on, holding her breath, forcing herself not to run. Round a corner she let out a big sigh and glanced back. No-one had followed; she hurried off.

She looked at the Dye Shed. It was so dark and dank - did she really work all those years in that smell and heat? She wished with all her heart that she had kept better friends with her fellow workers. Standing at the entrance, she saw the girls were taking off their aprons, getting ready to go home. She stopped a young lass:

'Is Moss here?'

The girl looked her up and down, then pointed into the darkness, and went off. Ren stared into the mass of bodies, chatting and moving with ease. She spotted Moss but held back - what if she refused to help?

'Some of us want to get home.' A young woman pushed past her, then stopped:

'Ren? Is it you?'

A little knot of women halted around her.

'I, I've come to see Moss.'

'Moss! Someone to see you.' The young woman watched with interest as Moss came forward:

'Ren?'

'Oh Moss!' Ren put her arms out. All the women gazed at her patchy Blue Hands.

Ren blushed, folding her arms inside her cloak: 'I need your help.'

Moss looked at Ren as if weighing up choices. Ren turned to go.

'Wait a moment.' Moss gathered a bag and cloak, took Ren's arm and walked out of the shed, leaving staring eyes and mutterings behind them. Ren began to speak.

'Quiet,' Moss hissed. 'You can't trust anyone nowadays.'

They walked further off, then Ren began in low tones:

'I'm sorry to cause trouble. Can you help me?'

Moss frowned: 'What about your friends at the Hall?'

'I have information for the Gild. I need to tell Vetch.'

Moss looked at her, then said:

'There's a back room at the Shebble Inn. The Gild use it for meetings.'

'Thank you, Moss.'

They walked on. Ren longed to blurt out her worries, but Moss's silence deterred her. As they walked, more Guards were up ahead in the square. Moss steered her away down a side alley.

On the quayside stood a two-storey inn. Its lights shone out into the dusk of evening. Moss took her in the back door and spoke to a red-faced man with side whiskers:

'Evening, Dogfish. Is the back room free tonight?'

'It is, young lady.'

'Good. Vetch is calling a Gild meeting.'

'Very well. Will you be wanting vittals? The missus has made rabbit stew and herb dumplings.'

Ren nodded at Moss, her stomach growling.

'That'll do. And small beer for the meeting. Many thanks, Dogfish.'

Moss opened a door to a room where a log fire burned. There were two long tables with benches either side. She sat Ren down and pointed to her hands.

'What's this?'

Ren blushed: 'A poor disguise, against spies.'

Moss shrugged: 'We hear rumours.'

'I'm sorry I haven't spoken before,' Ren confessed.

Moss shrugged again:

'I'll tell Vetch you're here. Don't worry.' She gave a brief smile.

Ren ate thankfully, and after a plateful with extra dumplings (that Mrs Dogfish insisted on: 'Anything for that lovely Vetch. He's a good lad') and a glass of small beer, feeling warm and full, she dozed in front of the fire.

Voices woke her; Vetch came in with Moss and two men. They eyed her curiously, but were polite:

'Evening, Miss.'

The men wore leather jerkins and loose linen trousers, with red bandannas that marked out all the workers in the Shebble trade. Vetch introduced them:

'Tern, he represents the Shebblers. Ash, the Mixers and Moss you know, she represents the Dye girls. All members of the Gild.' He turned to them: 'This is my sister, Ren.'

They nodded to her. Tern, a big man with broad shoulders, smiled at her:

'I knew your father. A grand man. You have a look of him about you.' He put out a hand, large and scarred. She shook it and smiled.

Vetch sat down: 'We're just waiting for Master Greenweed.'

Ren blanched: 'Oh, but surely -' She stood up. 'Vetch, I can't. He'll tell the Council.'

'Don't fret. Master Greenweed's first loyalty is to the Gild. He won't betray you.'

She sat, twisting a strand of hair, thinking about her last meeting with Greenweed at the Gild. Dogfish brought the beers:

'Evening gentlemen, ladies. Was the rabbit to your liking, miss?'

She smiled, nodding, then started at two smart raps on the door. Dogfish opened it and bowed his head:

'Master Greenweed, welcome.'

Greenweed wore a heavy cloak over a dark green wool jacket, the sleeves slashed with deep blue. He greeted each one by name and a shake of the hand. Last, he stood before Ren. He eyed her keenly:

'Good evening, Ren.'

With Vetch's encouragement she recounted the story of Bark's arrival with the Azurro and Chapbook. She blushed, looking over at Moss. Ren explained Lilac's words about the Mazards and how they would help the workers, and she added her own discovery in the Hall Library, what she'd read about Samara, a huge country with great resources of Azurro that made a high quality blue dye that could outshine and challenge the Shebble shell dye of Calico.

Tern and Ash exchanged glances, looking concerned. She omitted the fact that she'd freed Bark or where he and the Azurro were hidden, but she explained he could read the Chapbook, and seemed to have a family connection with Samara, so she suspected his motives. Master Greenweed listened and watched her with great concentration.

'I made a vow of silence to the Mazards, but, but my first loyalty is to the Blue Hands.' Tears filled her eyes, her chest heaved: 'I have been followed, questioned, and,' her tears fell and she sobbed, 'threatened with my life.' And betrayed too, she thought. Her heart was bitter as she remembered Lilac's letter, and she shed more tears.

Moss put an arm around her. The men exclaimed:

'Who threatened you?'

'Grist, the Governor's man?' Vetch asked.

Ren nodded, wiping her eyes.

Greenweed's eyes flashed:

'That's no way to conduct Council business. The Governor seems to forget he's elected to govern on our behalf, not his. He goes his own way too much.'

Ren was surprised to hear Master Greenweed criticise the

Governor.

'A breach of Article 5?' Vetch argued. 'That's no light matter. Is it any wonder he's acting with an iron hand, to root out the Mazards?'

The others nodded.

Tern frowned: 'What are the Samarans up to? How do we know this foreign dye's quality?'

'It could destroy our whole industry,' Ash said.

'We must protect our workers.' Moss spoke for the first time.

'That is our first, our only priority!' Tern thumped the table with his large fist.

'But how?' Vetch gave them all a searching stare.

'Destroy the Azurro.' 'Hunt down the foreigner.' 'Prosecute and punish the Mazards. Suppress this dangerous idea.' They were all speaking at once. Master Greenweed raised a hand:

'We must act with care and think this through. We can't prosecute the Lady Lilac ourselves.'

'No, but we can show our disapproval.' Moss's eyes blazed.

'Aye, remind the merchants and Governor that we have a view.'

'Yes, a power of our own.' Vetch made a fist. 'We should plan a march. A show of strength. All the Blue Hands together.'

'Aye,' 'Yes,' the others agreed. Greenweed looked thoughtful:

'Yes, perhaps that would be right. However, we don't know what the Mazards have formally been accused of or what hard evidence the authorities have.'

Ren had been taking in all the arguments, glad she'd done right by the Blue Hands. Moss turned to her:

'If Ren speaks out, they'll have evidence enough, surely?'

Chapter 8
The Alchemist

Ren stuttered, 'Oh, but - it's one thing to tell you, here, in secret. To stand in public and - oh.' She put her hands to her face. 'No, no. I can't.'

Tern looked at her: 'We'll support you.' Vetch and the other men agreed.

'But, I ..' She shook her head.

'Don't worry, sister. It may not come to that,' Vetch reassured her, but now it had been said it seemed the only possible outcome. She'd have to confess her own part in hiding the Azurro, and it would mean betraying Bark too.

They continued to discuss what the Gild should do. The Master urged caution and patience:

'Dyers don't add the fixer till the mix is right.'

'Ah, but the wise weaver checks his threads *before* they snap!' Ash wagged a finger. The others nodded and agreed that a march should be planned.

'It's late.' Master Greenweed rose. 'Thank you, my dear. You have done the right thing.'

The men left. Vetch and Moss hovered:

'You can stay here. Safe for tonight. What about tomorrow?'

'I suppose I must return to the Barrow Hall. Face what must be faced.'

'Well done.' Vetch hugged her. 'I'm proud to call you sister.'

She smiled and kissed him goodnight. Moss gave her a hug and a long searching look. She tried to smile, miserable as they left.

Mrs Dogfish led her upstairs with a candle and showed her into a tiny room, with a bed that folded down from behind cupboard doors.

'Tis small, but I think you'll be comfortable. Goodnight, my dear.'

She lit a rush light and left. Ren took off her dirty outer clothes, uncoiled her hair and lay down in her shift. Tiredness made her limbs heavy; she wanted to think but her eyes were closing. She blew out the light and fell straight asleep.

She awoke sometime later to a flame floating at the end of her bed. It flickered and moved in the pitch dark. She blinked her eyes and clutched the bed cover:

'Who's there?' she cried.

She made out a figure, cloaked and masked. Her insides turned liquid.

'Quiet,' said a man's voice, muffled by the mask.

Her mouth dry, she couldn't speak. She sat up, heart pumping, preparing to fight or run if she could.

'Bark is free. You know where he's hiding, don't you?'

The words hung in the air between them. Ren clutched the bed cover tighter.

Was this a trap? Had she been betrayed?

The figure moved. Ren flinched: 'Stay back!'

'Time's short.'

He stood at the end of her bed, too close in the small room:

'Bring him to me. I want the plant, also.'

'I don't know what you're talking about.' Her voice wavered in the dark.

'I'm the Alchemist.'

She took a breath. How had he found her? Who else was watching her?

'The Mazards do no good,' she challenged him.

'Neither does the Governor..'

She drew back as the masked face leaned towards her.

'I won't harm you.'

His shadow loomed up the wall. Trembling, she shook her head.

'Bark's life is at risk.' He said again: 'I won't harm you.'

She stared at the masked face.

Could she trust him? She wanted to believe someone could protect Bark.

'Here.' He dropped a small leather pouch at the end of the bed. It chinked. 'This will buy food and other necessaries.'

Ren stared at the pouch.

'Be sure to bring him to the landing below the Shebble Inn at midnight, two days from now. There'll be no moon. A boat'll be waiting.'

The figure had gone before Ren could ask any more. She reached out, took the pouch and tiptoed to the window. All she saw was the deserted quayside, a little glimmer of moonlight on the water, dark boats shifting at their moorings.

Next morning, Ren slipped out at dawn, aware of her dirty clothes. In the harbour, fishermen were coming in with the night's catch; at the market, yawning stall-holders were putting out their wares. The air smelt of fresh fish. How had the Alchemist known where to find her? Her head told her she must support the Gild yet in her heart she wanted to help Bark. As she neared the Hall, she walked slower. What should she tell Lilac? The letter to Bark burned in her pocket. Growing hot and agitated, Ren walked through the alleys leading to the Barrow Hall, planning her words.

At the door of the Hall a Guard looked her up and down, barring her way:

'Grist's bin looking for you.'

'Then let me through.'

'He's angry. Wants a *conversation*. In his private room.'

Ren's eyes widened, but she said nothing. He pushed her forwards. She resisted:

'I must see to my Lady.'

'She can wait.'

'I'll get him information. Tonight, the Great Hall. I promise.'

'It'll be my neck if you don't.' He let her go.

She hastened up to her own room, took Lilac's letter for Bark and shoved it in the drawer under her bed, along with the money pouch. She caught her breath and calmed herself, changed out of her dirty clothes and set off to face Lilac.

The Guard at the door nodded. She knocked and entered. Lilac, looking pale, sprang up from a chair.

'Where have you been? I'm imprisoned here with no news, no-one to speak to for days!'

Ren stood facing Lilac, her hands clasped tight:

'I went to my mother's.'

'Your mother's! Again?'

Ren shook her head, put a finger to her lips and gestured, then said loudly: 'My Lady, you look pale, let us walk in the courtyard.'

She opened the door and spoke to the Guard:

'My Lady needs fresh air.'

'Well, I suppose it'll be all right.'

Lilac snapped: 'I won't run away.'

They went downstairs, the Guard following. Ren stiffened as Lilac took her arm, walking the footpaths between grassy rectangles and flower beds. The mid-morning sun beat down, the Guard stood in the shade.

Ren described how she had freed Bark:

'We were all but drowned, my Lady. And his left arm.'

Lilac paled. 'Yes?'

'It hung useless, I had to -' Ren shuddered at the memory, 'put it right.'

Lilac gave a little gulping sob: 'And my letter?'

Without knowing what she would reply, out it came:

'It got wet and destroyed in the flood my Lady. He never saw it.'

Lilac walked silently, taking it all in, then she hugged Ren's arm to her:

'Well done, Ren. I can't thank you enough.'

Ren flushed, with a mixture of triumph and guilt. Then Lilac whispered:

'Where's Bark now?'

'In hiding, my Lady,' Ren said.

She wouldn't tell Lilac where, nor about meeting the Alchemist either.

The Guard marched them back and Ren went to fetch bread, cheese and plums from the kitchen. Cook said nothing as he handed her the food. There was a tense atmosphere in the Hall. All were unsettled by the rumour of spies everywhere, watching everyone.

She set down the plate of food. Ren watched Lilac's lips open, the way her hands moved, how her tongue licked her fingers; she thought of Bark's fingers touching Lilac. Hating the pull of her own desires, she couldn't hold back, she had to ask:

'How did you meet with Bark in Braymer?'

'At a special gathering.'

'What about?'

'To discuss trade routes around the cosmos.'

Ren stuttered over her question: 'Is that when you and Bark - formed the Mazards?'

'What is this Ren, are you the inquisitor now?'

'Oh no! On my heart's blood.'

She took the plates and left. I'm becoming like them, she told herself. Perhaps that was the only way to survive, caught up in their plots. Was she going to comply with the Alchemist's demand that she bring Bark to him? And what would she to say to Grist tonight?

Bundling up her muddy clothes, she went down to the washhouse, where a copper boiler was always full. As she plunged and scrubbed the chemise and skirt, memories of

Bark filled her mind. She thought of them lying together and kissing. She tasted his lips again. As she sweated with the scrubbing and wringing out, she breathed his name into the steamy air, imagining his brown skin on hers, his hands on her body. She knew one thing for certain: she'd get him to the Alchemist tomorrow night, away from Grist's hands, keep him safe, alive. Keep him for herself.

As she hung the damp clothes out, she wondered how to deal with Grist and what she'd say to him. Perhaps Lady Rose would help.

She found Rose in the upstairs Lesser Hall, a long room with a low ceiling. Shutters were open to the courtyard, so a cool breeze could circulate. This is where ladies and maids gathered to share such pastimes as embroidery or play music. Lilac never participated in these events, claiming the conversation was tedious, and she felt stifled.

Ren stood at the door: a young woman was plucking a soulful tune on the mandora, while a group of ladies worked on a large tapestry frame together. Lady Rose sat a little apart wafting a fan, her own embroidery frame idle in front of her.

'My Lady, I have nothing to occupy my time. May I assist you?'

Rose looked at her, suspicion in her eyes. She nodded. Ren sat at the frame and pulled out the needle. She followed a line of neat stitches, shaping a bird's yellow wing. Rose watched to assess her ability.

'My Lady.' Ren spoke in a low voice so others wouldn't hear, 'I am afraid for my life.'

She hadn't intended to say that, but it had an instant effect on Lady Rose who sat up and leaned forward.

'I have been threatened, and ill-used. By Grist... because..'

Lady Rose pulled her chair a little closer.

Ren drew the thread through and pierced the cloth again, making another stitch. She whispered:

'My Lady's a member of a secret society.'

Rose listened intently. As Ren made a line of yellow feathers with the needle, she explained how Lilac had recruited her to the Mazards and she told Rose about Azurro.

'When Grist arrested Lilac and tortured Bark,' she stammered, 'and ..couldn't get what he wanted, he turned to me.' She kept her head down so her words were mumbled:

'I've agreed to meet him. Tonight. I'm afraid ..he may.. *force me to speak.*' She pricked herself with the needle. 'Ow!' She sucked her finger.

The music stopped, the other ladies were casting glances in their direction.

Rose beckoned a servant over with a jug. He poured a glass of lemon water, then retreated into the shadows discreetly. The music began again.

Offered the glass, Ren took a sip and breathed. Lady Rose snapped her fan open and cooled herself.

'I don't wish to be disloyal. Nor do anything improper.' Ren drank her lemon water.

'Yet you acted illegally?'

'As you told me to.' Ren looked at Rose out of the corner of her eye.

Rose fanned a little faster. 'Perhaps the court will

understand.'

'Will you accompany me, to my appointment with Grist? As my witness?'

Lady Rose held the fan still, frowning. Ren bent to the sewing again, finishing a wing tip. She looked up, Rose gave her the faintest nod, and leaned forward over the embroidery frame:

'You have left a spot of blood on my bird.'

After sharing an evening meal of fish stew with Lilac, Ren retired to her room. Lady Rose appeared at the appointed time in a cloak, wearing a feathered mask Ren thought a little extreme. They went down to the Great Hall, gloomy with only a few candles lit. Their footsteps echoed in the empty space. Grist appeared from behind a pillar.

'What's she doing here?'

'My protection.'

He grunted: 'Who is it?'

'No names. That's her protection.'

He gave a low laugh: 'Think you're clever, playing me at my own game?' He came closer. 'Don't waste my time. Where've you been?'

Ren cleared her throat: 'To visit my mother.' She glanced briefly at Rose, 'My Lady gave me permission.'

'Where's that?'

What could she say? He'd find out anyway. 'East, by the allotments.'

He grunted: 'What's this information you have for me?'

Ren began a long explanation: how Lilac went to Braymer

and met Bark, who was from Samara. She began to describe where Samara was.

'Yes, yes!' Grist was impatient. 'I know where it is.'

When she described Azurro, Grist's eyes gleamed. This was something he didn't know. She gave an elaborate account of how they formed the Mazards with Charlatan.

'I knew he was part of it,' Grist interjected. 'Mazards you say?'

'Yes, and they made me carry a message at the May Day Revels from Bark to Lilac. They enjoined me to silence, but they tell me nothing.'

'I caught them all in your room.'

'They thought you wouldn't think to look there. Under your nose, they said.'

'Ha - idiots. So you don't know where he is now?'

'Who?' Ren acted surprised.

'Someone freed Bark from the 'gettory.'

Ren shook her head. 'My Lady said nothing to me.'

'What about the rest of this Azurro?'

'I saw it on the actors' ship, The Starfish.' With an earnest expression, she turned to Rose: 'It's the truth.'

'The Starfish has left Calico.' Lady Rose spoke up. 'You can't expect this young girl to know everything.'

Grist nodded. 'You'll have to repeat it under oath. At the court hearing.' He melted back into the shadows.

Lady Rose gathered her cloak and marched off. Ren followed whispering:

'Thank you, thank you my Lady.'

Rose turned to her: 'You mention my part in this to no-one.' Rose nipped her for good measure and left without a backward glance.

Ren sat on her bed, her pulse racing - she'd betrayed her Mistress, with Rose's knowledge and consent. It went against everything that Rose had taught her. She supposed there weren't any rules of etiquette for spies and criminals. No wonder Rose insisted she never speak of it. She closed her eyes. Did she feel remorse, or sorrow for Lilac? No, she deserved her fate. Ren had acted according to her conscience.

It seemed like years since she'd become Lilac's maid and go-between. She'd saved a life, had her life threatened, told lies and met Bark - the world was going at the speed of a mill race. Did she still want to return to the Dye Sheds? She lay back and let the thought drift.

She'd burnt her boats as far as Lilac was concerned. The honest way was to tell her what she'd done, then leave. She'd do it first thing tomorrow. It might give her just the excuse she needed.

Next morning, after breakfast, she stood outside Lilac's door, patted her hair, pulled her skirts then made her expression as neutral as she could. Inside she hovered, wanting to speak and not sure how to start:

'My Lady, there are chores I have been neglecting.'

Lilac waved a hand: 'They can wait a bit longer. I want a book. Travels of a Calico Captain.'

Ren's hair roots tingled. She nodded and went off.

She returned with it, held in both hands, not offering it to

Lilac, and asked:

'Is it - informative?'

'Yes, very. I need to prepare for the court hearing. I want you to help me.' Lilac put out her hand. Ren held the book tight to her chest.

'I must anticipate every question they may ask and decide how best to answer.' Lilac held her hand out again:

'They've evidence but no witnesses. I want to -'

'My Lady, there's something I have to tell you.' Ren gripped the book, blushing deep red, not meeting Lilac's eyes: 'I've spoken to Grist.'

Lilac's expression went blank.

'I've agreed to be a witness.' Ren held up her chin, her hands trembled, knuckles white.

Lilac's eyes grew dark as storm clouds.

'My Lady, you know I had doubts about Azurro.'

'Perhaps you don't know enough to decide?' Lilac was icy.

Ren held the book up. 'I've read this!'

Lilac tried to grab the book from her: 'We only work to *help* the Blue Hands!'

Holding the book out of Lilac's reach, Ren said: 'I don't believe you.'

Lilac grabbed again: 'You say I'm lying?'

Ren hesitated, not sure of her answer, but still not letting go of the book.

'Ha!' Lilac pointed at Ren. 'You've hidden the Azurro, you helped Bark!'

Ren hung her head, silent. Lilac snatched the book, Ren let it go.

Lilac waved it in Ren's face, 'One book doesn't make you an expert.'

Ren flushed: 'I know what I've seen! I won't do it anymore.'

Lilac's mouth dropped open. She glared at Ren, incensed: 'You're an ignorant young woman!'

'You're not honest with me!' Ren shouted.

'You wouldn't understand.'

Ren exploded: 'You never offered me the opportunity to understand!'

Lilac stamped her foot, shouting: 'I've offered you so much, Ren! So much, and you reward me like this?'

'You've used me!'

'No! You chose to join the Mazards.'

'I'm a Lady's maid.' Ren choked with anger. Her whole body shook, 'How could I have refused? Now I must act according to my conscience.'

'Fine words, but spoken by a fool,' Lilac spat. 'I dismiss you from my service. I think you'd better leave.'

'Willingly.' Ren's eyes narrowed.

Lilac turned away: 'Get out of my sight!'

Ren had no breath and nothing to say. She turned and burst out of the room, surprising the Guard who had his ear to the door.

'What's going on?' he called, but Ren no longer cared. She ran straight to her chamber, eyes stinging with tears. As she grabbed a few things to pack a bag, she found Lilac's letter. It was limp and still smelt faintly of vanilla. She ripped it into tiny shreds, muttering:

'Let her rot, curse her!'

Tonight it would be the dark of the moon: she'd take Bark to the Alchemist. After that she didn't care. Down in the kitchen, ignoring the questioning eyes of the staff, she found a basket, put in two apples, some cheese and two bread rolls. She filled a leather water bottle from the icy barrel in the pantry. At the door, she flinched as the latch snapped open. Out in the alley, she hastened away before anyone could stop her. Confessing to Grist wouldn't be the end of it, his men would be watching, waiting. Avoiding open spaces, she zigzagged a route down to the quayside and looked around for a rowing boat to fetch Bark.

A golden morning light bathed the town; the horizon was hazy. As she stood there breathing fast, the realisation hit her.

The Azurro in the chook house!

She clenched her fists in frustration. What now? Could she leave it? No, that wasn't fair to her family. To be rid of it, that was best. She looked around. She'd have to go home to collect it, then get back to the harbour, all in broad daylight, carrying the sack! She felt sick as she made her way to the allotments, clutching her basket, stopping at corners to take a quick glance around before carrying on.

Chapter 9
Husher Cove

A number of neighbours were weeding their patches and tending to plants. Some raised their heads and nodded as she walked by. She loitered, picking at leaves and pretending to examine flowers. The chooks were out, pecking in the dirt. She knelt to the coop and looked inside. Empty! She put a hand in and felt around - nothing. Her heart stopped.

'Lookin' for eggs?'

She cracked her skull on the door frame in her rush to turn. It was her mother's friend, old Pa Hodden.

'Won't find much. Your mother says they ent laying.'

She looked up at him, rubbing the back of her head.

'No. Gone broody or summit. And my goosegogs got blight, more's the pity. Had a lovely crop last year. Lovely!'

She stood, nodding at his words.

'How you finding it up at the Hall? We all very proud of yer. First Blue Hand a Lady's maid. Well, whatever next, I said. She'll look prettier 'n a daisy in pink, I said. You always was the best looking girl round here. He he.' He chuckled. 'What's in your basket - Herd cheese? An they looks like Calico Reds, them apples. They feed you well up there, do they?'

Ren backed away, still nodding:

'Yes, thanks…I must..' she turned, his words following her down the path.

'My taties are coming along nice if your ma wants some!'

She waved and hurried away.

At the corner of her lane, she saw two strangers at the door speaking to her mother. She flattened herself against a wall and waited, listening to the pounding of her blood. She screwed up her eyes and cursed. What was she thinking of, getting her mother into trouble? This was all her fault!

She risked a quick look; one man was still at the door, as she watched the other came out. Her mother was talking and pointing away down the path. The two men left. She waited, counting to ten. Could she risk it, would they come back? She counted to ten again then took another look. No sign of them. She came out from behind the wall and hurried to the front door, still open. She listened a moment, then tiptoed inside, startling her mother.

'Ren!?'

'Who were those two men?'

'From the Hall. Looking for something.'

'Me?'

'They didn't say.'

Ren sat with her basket in her lap, fingering the apples.

'My Lady has dismissed me.'

Her mother sat beside her, put a hand on her back.

Ren asked: 'Will they come back?'

Her mother shrugged. Ren leant against her mother's shoulder.

'I'm sorry. Bringing trouble to you, Ma. I think - I know what those men were looking for. I hid something. Something - important. Now - it's gone.'

She covered her face with her hands and let out a groan.

Her mother took her hand:

'Come with me.' She led her back to the allotment. Pa

120

Hodden was hoeing. He smiled as they approached.

'Can we borrow the wheel cart?' Fern asked him.

'Why, o'course.'

From round behind the fruit bushes he pulled the wooden hand cart, full of spiky gooseberry cuttings. As Ren looked closer she could see something buried underneath, like a canvas sack.

'Where would you be wanting it?' He smiled.

Ren wept with relief, embracing her mother.

'It was upsetting the chooks, so we moved it. Quite heavy, it was.'

'I'm sorry.' She said into her mother's arms. 'I should have said something.'

Her mother patted her back. 'Now. What's to be done with it?'

Ren dried her eyes, thinking fast. She asked Pa Hodden:

'Can you wheel it to the harbour for me? I've coins to pay you.'

'No need. Happy to help.'

She flushed: 'I'll take a separate route, just in case...'

'Righty ho, me dear.' He chuckled.

Her mother held her back and gave her a questioning look.

'It's all right - I'll be - all right.'

Ren met him on the quayside, where she'd hired a rowing boat with the Alchemist's purse. Pa Hodden fished out the sack and carried it down to her. She pressed a coin into his calloused hand and kissed his cheek.

'Prettiest girl of the lot.' He chuckled and climbed to the

quayside. 'You take care now.' He ambled off, pushing his cart, whistling.

Untying the painter, she dropped her basket into the boat beside the sack, sat down and took a deep breath. There was comfort in the familiar smell of a tarry, salty vessel - she was released from the confinement of the Hall, on a journey of her own at last. She looked around, no-one seemed to be taking any notice of her. It had been a long time since she'd handled a boat. The heavy wooden oars were awkward to lift and manoeuvre; she struggled to fit them into the rowlocks. Readying herself, she braced her feet and heaved, feeling the strain on her back and arms as she rowed away from the quayside, forcing the wood against the water, praying no-one would stop her.

Out of the harbour walls she sighed in relief and smiled at the thought of Bark waiting at the end of her journey. There wasn't a breath of wind, the sea was calm and flat as a pond, the sun was a warm hand on her back. She pulled at the oars, finding her rhythm, skimming the little boat through the pale blue inshore waters. Gold sunlight bouncing off the sea dazzled her as she worked, bending and stretching. Her arms complained but she rowed steadily. Beads of sweat trickled down her forehead and her underarms showed dark patches. She enjoyed the freedom, the power of her muscles, in control, alive, at no-one's beck and call. Now she had one thought in her head - Bark.

By late morning she rounded a spit and Husher Cove came into view. It looked deserted, and she pulled the oars, trailing first the left, then the right, to angle the boat into the channel. She couldn't help banging against the rock sides, but worked her way up to the top of the inlet. As she stood to tie up to a ring, she noticed the sack of Azurro. She'd forgotten all about it, and her idea of throwing it away. Using the rope, she hauled herself onto the rocks, leaving the basket and Azurro behind.

She'd find Bark first.

The steps in the cliff were in shadow, she bounded up until she reached the grassy ledge, pink and breathless, and ran along, lifting the draping greenery to enter the tunnel. Hands covered her eyes from behind, making her gasp, and set her stomach buzzing.

'You make enough noise to waken the dead, Ren.'

She laughed and swung round to see Bark, gaunt and unshaven, full of uncertainty.

'I wasn't sure you'd come back.' He searched her face. She kissed him in answer.

He returned her kiss, murmuring: 'My fearless seabird.'

She pulled away, to catch her breath:

'How's your arm?'

'Getting better. Much better now you've arrived.'

'Are you hungry? I've food.' She gestured to the boat.

'Starving.'

They climbed down to the harbour together and Ren clambered into the boat and handed up the basket.

Back up on the grassy ledge, Ren leant against Bark while he ate; every action he took, sinuous and graceful, thrilled her. She was glad he'd be safe.

'The Alchemist contacted me. I'm to bring you to the harbour, tonight.'

'Ah. At last.' Bark looked pleased. 'So you delivered my message?'

'No. He just appeared in my room one night.'

They sat looking out to sea, both wrapped in their own thoughts.

'Grist's angry you've escaped.'

Bark laughed.

'I'm frightened of him. Of what he might do. To you. And me.'

'You frightened? I don't believe it.' Bark reached up and touched her cheek.

'There's going to be a court hearing,' Ren said. 'I'll have to give evidence.'

She shifted and looked away.

'You wouldn't betray me?' He put an arm around her. She pushed him away. He held her tighter and kissed her.

'Things will be for the better, you'll see. This Azurro..'

'It's not just the Azurro!' she cried.

Bark stopped smiling: 'You're angry with me?'

'What about you and my Lady?' Ren couldn't stop herself.

'Lilac?' He seemed puzzled.

'She wrote you a love letter!' Ren accused. 'I never delivered it.'

'I'm accused of not receiving a letter?' Bark laughed. He put his hand on her shoulders and pulled her round; she didn't resist.

'Don't be jealous, Ren, it spoils a woman.' He looked her

in the eyes, leaned forward and kissed her softly.

Another accusation tumbled out: 'You're from Samara!'

After a long pause he said: 'Yes.'

Ren stood up, furious, 'You lied!'

'No.'

'You don't support the Blue Hands!?'

Bark rubbed his forehead: 'Ren. Listen.'

'You're not from Calico or Braymer. How can you care about us?' She threw her arms wide. 'Your country is so big - it could destroy our Islands and our people!'

'That is what we -'

'We?'

'The Mazards, are trying to avoid. We want peaceful trade, to the benefit of all.'

'You lied to me,' she insisted.

'No, just withheld some of the truth.'

She folded her arms and turned away, staring out to sea.

'Many people will react as you've done once they know I'm from Samara.'

'You play with words.' And with me, she thought.

He caught her hand, pulled her down.

'Believe me, I like it here. I like the people.'

He kissed her, his lips tasted of apple. Ren couldn't think straight anymore. She didn't want to argue with him. She wished they could stay in this little cove and forget all about the Mazards.

She put her arms around his neck, returning his kisses, fired by the conflict churning inside her. She lay back and pulled him down, her embrace fierce with desire edged with anger. Her tongue slid in between his lips. She took his hand and put it on her breast, he fingered her nipple, making it tight and hard. Lines of sensation ran through her as she pushed her hips towards him.

She was breathing fast and shallow. His hand was on her ankle, he slid it slowly up her shin, lifting her skirt, he rested it on her knee, then began moving slowly further up. She groaned, and pulled at the buckles and ties of his breeches, kissing him over and over.

He stopped.

She half-opened her eyes, caught in the moment, as if her limbs had abandoned her.

'This isn't right.' Bark sat up, his mood had shifted.

She waited, confused and breathless.

'Is it Lilac?' She put a hand out to him.

He stood and walked away.

'No. This isn't right. For many reasons. I don't want to use you.'

Her mood evaporated. She sat up.

'Oh, yes. I know people use me, and then they throw me aside. Lilac has dismissed me, and now you. Once I've done the Mazards' dirty work, I'm just a useless Nobody!'

Bark's face fell, he came back and knelt beside her:

'No. I didn't mean that.'

'It's the truth, isn't it?'

'No - no.'

She hardened her heart, closing herself off from him. He put a hand on her shoulder. She shrugged it off. She hated him! She hated herself for being so ridiculous. She blushed an angry red and hid her face, clasping her drawn-up knees.

To cool down and regain her composure, she got up and walked away. The little cove was still and turquoise. She climbed down to the harbour. The water had risen nearly level with the rocks. She sat and dangled her legs in the water; tiny fish darted to and fro, she watched the sun shaping and reshaping patterns on the water. Throwing off her dress, she swam in her under clothes, cooling herself in the sea. Her hair floated like soft weed.

* * *

As they waited for dark, imagining the miles of ocean between Calico and Samara, Ren asked:

'That story - about the big country and the prophecy - was that about Samara?'

'Yes.'

'And the stranger on the ship - did he write Travels of a Calico Captain?'

'Yes - you know it? It was a way of trying to explain. The cosmos is opening up. Explorers are navigating routes across the oceans. Think what could be learnt, discovered and exchanged. This is how the world should be!' His eyes flashed.

'But why doesn't Samara use Azurro as a dye?'

'We do - all over the country.'

'So why don't you export it, like we do with Shebble?'

'My country is vast - you cannot imagine. The Overlord rules it all in name, but there are many Underlords. They rule their lands with independence. Samarans are a fierce people, many are nomadic. We do not have Gilds and ordered structures like little Calico.'

'But if it's so big, why aren't you really powerful?'

'We are. But we're like a slumbering giant. We're backward in many ways, with much to learn from your country.'

'And what does the king of Samara think?'

He paused and smiled: 'My father is beginning to think as I do.'

Ren's mouth dropped open: 'Your father..?'

'Overlord, we don't use the word king.' Bark smiled.

'I'm in disgrace back home.' Bark laughed, 'Or I was. I think things are changing in my country.' He looked away out to sea.

She sat silent, considering the implications, blushing, and wanted to ask him a hundred questions, but time was running out.

They sat just inside the tunnel entrance, and discussed the arrangements for the night. Ren would row Bark to the harbour, as his arm wasn't healed yet. He would meet with the Alchemist, and take the Azurro with him.

'What will the Alchemist do with the plant?'

'He wants to see if he can mix the dye, here on Calico.'

Ren shook her head: 'The Gild'll fight against it. And when it comes to a fight, I support the Blue Hands.'

Bark looked at her. 'So why are you taking me there?'

She plaited her hair and pinned it up. 'For your own protection.' She gave him the Alchemist's money pouch and refused to take it back.

Watching the last rays of sun tip the clouds with orange and red, Bark pressed Ren where she'd go after tonight.

'I'll simply tie the boat back where I got it.'

'Then what?'

'Go home.' She shrugged.

Bark said nothing.

Ren checked that they had the basket and water bottle ready to load into the boat.

'We must leave soon.'

'It's hard to know time with no moon.' Bark stood up and scanned the twilight. He froze and gripped Ren's arm.

'Ssh.' He pointed.

Ren looked down and, lit by the last rays of the sun, she saw a boat had rowed into the harbour. Two dark shapes were moving, searching, coming up the cliff.

'Into the tunnel.' Ren pulled Bark and they crept back until the curtain of greenery hid them. They listened and waited. Footsteps came nearer - a soft padding. These men were trying not to be seen or heard. They stepped off the path and explored the ledge a little way. If they found the tunnel entrance, she and Bark would be trapped with no way down to sea level, their boat and escape. They had to be distracted. Ren squeezed to the furthest reaches of the tunnel. She cupped her hands to her mouth and called: 'Halloo!'

A narrow ventilation shaft opened up and out at the cliff top. A trick of nature made her cry echo up the shaft and emerge at the cliff top. She whispered:

'We did this as children. It might work.'

She called again, her heart beating. The men outside

exchanged a few hurried words, then their footsteps padded away, up the path to the top of the cliff.

'Now,' Bark urged. Grabbing the basket and water bottle, they scrambled down to their boat. Ren jumped in, he dropped the basket and leather bottle at her feet, untied both painters and threw himself down as Ren pulled the oars. They towed the other boat and pushed it out to sea. They were into open water when they heard the cry of anger as they left Husher Cove, and the men, far behind.

'You come to my rescue once again, fearless seabird.'

She ignored his smile: 'If they're on foot, we'll arrive well before them.'

The sky was thick with stars. They rounded the spit and headed east towards the harbour. The wind picked up, rocking the boat, cold spray hit them from the waves. Ren pulled hard, her muscles stiff from the morning. Bark's eyes watched her as she bent and stretched, admiring the strength of her limbs, the rhythm of her body.

'You handle a boat like a sailor.' Bark said.

She smiled but said nothing. Within an hour and a half, they were outside the harbour walls.

'We need to go quietly,' Bark whispered. She nodded.

'I can feather.' She held the oar flat to the water once she'd made the rowing stroke. The blade sliced through the air, silent as a bird's wing.

They floated into the harbour, Bark keeping a lookout. Ren pulled the boat into the quay wall, and grabbed onto a wet rope that hung down, slimy with weed. She could hear

Bark's breathing, the water lap, and further, the faint boom of the waves onto the shoreline along the coast. She reached out and took his hand in the dark. They sat silent, together, waiting.

After a while, she saw a cloaked figure on the quay beside the Shebble Inn. A boat rowed across the harbour to the landing below it.

'There.' She whispered. 'I hope this isn't another trap.'

She pulled away from the quay wall and rowed toward the landing, drawing up alongside the boat moored there:

'Are you for Alchemy?' a voice asked.

'Alchemy and Freedom,' replied Bark.

'Welcome Mazard.'

After this exchange of words, the cloaked figure descended from the quayside and stepped into the first boat. Ren held the two boats together as Bark handed over the bag of Azurro, and stepped in beside the cloaked figure.

The Alchemist turned to Ren: 'Thank you.'

Bark reached out and put his hand to her cheek: 'Take care.'

She covered his hand with her own, for a brief moment, then he was gone.

The three men rowed off.

Ren sat rocking gently on the inky water, watching Bark slip into darkness. She was tired - tired of running and hiding, tired of fear, of carrying messages for others, tired of the confusion in her heart and mind. She wanted to be safe, for it all to stop, the constant thoughts whirling round - who to trust, what to do.

She had no way of knowing where Bark had gone and no idea if she would see him again. But there was one thing she was sure of: this was the last task she would undertake for the Mazards. And she wasn't going back to Lilac.

She tied up the boat and plodded home, glad of the dark so no-one would see her humiliation. She crept into the quiet house, curled up in her cloak on the floor and sank into sleep.

Chapter 10
Grist

She fell into a simple routine - helping her mother with household tasks, attending to the allotment, and running errands to the market. She assumed someone would call for her when the court hearing began. She avoided friends and neighbours, their enquiring eyes, their gossip and speculation.

She went to the allotment wearing an old skirt of her mother's and a sacking apron, and a shirt that no longer fitted Vetch. She'd roll up the sleeves and take the bucket of scraps for the pigs. She collected eggs from all the little hiding places that she remembered as a girl: under hedges, in long grass, wherever the wandering chooks decided to lay. Although she wore a reed hat, her skin, unused to the sun and exposure to the elements, turned a freckled honey-gold. She took a perverse delight in losing her pale looks: she looked like a worker, not a noble. She enjoyed it - physical work that left her tired but satisfied at the end of the day. It stopped her dwelling on the court hearing, though she often thought of Bark.

Vetch didn't ask her to come to any more Gild meetings. He went on his own, in the evenings, going round different groups of workers, discussing the march, planning tactics. He told her some of their intentions, and she listened, asking questions and making suggestions. They had meals together every evening, her mother happy to have them both close at hand. Ren found she didn't miss the Barrow Hall, but as soon as that thought took hold, she'd remember what lay ahead, and her stomach would sink.

One morning, shopping in the market, a rough hand pulled her up short:

'Well, well - Look who it is.'

'Let me pass!'

'I don't think you're going anywhere.' Grist produced a paper from inside his jerkin and waved it in her face.

'An arrest warrant with your name on it.'

'You... can't arrest me.'

'Oh, and why not? Who's to stop me?'

'I've told you all I know.'

'Liar!' He caught her wrist.

She twisted away, but Grist held on.

'How did pretty boy escape, eh?'

She pulled hard, but his grip was too tight

'Who helped him? Who was at Husher Cove the other night?'

She yanked her arm free and ran a few steps. He ran, grabbed her arm and whipped her cheek with the back of his hand. Ren fell and her face hit the ground with a loud crack. Heads turned, a small crowd gathered. Stunned and winded, she lay still. A woman cried:

'You've hurt her!'

He glared at the woman, who backed away.

'Oh, this isn't hurting..'

He bent down, caught a handful of Ren's hair, and hoisted

her up hard. She gasped. He pushed his face close up to hers. She smelt his fishy breath:

'She don't know what *hurting* is - yet.'

A big butcher hauled him off and gripped Grist by his jerkin:

'That's no way to treat a lass.'

A woman helped her sit up, saying:

'Are yer all right, honey?'

A little blood trickled from Ren's mouth. The woman tutted and wiped it with her apron.

Grist pushed the butcher away: 'Idiots. I'm arresting this woman.' He waved the paper.

The butcher snatched it out of his hands:

'How do we know it's official? What does it say?'

Grist snorted. He pointed to the Governor's stamp: 'You can see that even if you can't read.'

Ren rose unsteadily, holding the woman's arm. The crowd stood round, commenting:

'Look at her face!' 'Poor young lass.'

They turned on Grist, threatening:

'Who are you?'

'Not wearing a Barrow Guard uniform, is he?'

'Does the Governor know you hit women?'

'Oh dear!' The butcher crumpled the arrest warrant between meaty hands, 'Better get another one from the Governor.'

Grist was purple: 'What's your name?'

The butcher folded his arms: 'What's yours?'

Grist balled his fists and growled, but he was outnumbered:

'Bloody fools!'

He walked away followed by the crowd's jeers.

'Here, let me look at that face.' The butcher touched her cheek with his fingertips. She closed her eyes.

'Nothing broken, but you'll look like a strip of dyed cloth tomorrow.'

She began to sway.

'Here, sit a minute.' The woman led her to a bench. 'Just get your breath.'

Ren lowered herself onto the seat.

'Careful.' The woman held her steady. 'Where's yer home?'

'By the allotments.'

The butcher said: 'Wait here.'

'Arnica - that'll help.' She patted Ren's back

Five minutes later the butcher returned with a lanky lad pushing a hand cart.

'Larch says he'll take you home.'

Larch grinned, revealing a lack of front teeth. The woman and butcher lifted Ren into the cart, and Larch set off, head down, concentrating on avoiding pot holes.

When they stopped at her door, Larch helped her down.

She tried to smile, but her face didn't respond. Larch grinned his toothless grin and set off again. Ren stumbled to the house and put a hand on the door frame as her head swam. She collapsed to her knees; her mother cried:

'Oh my!'

She dabbed at the blood on Ren's lips, tutting all the while: 'What a thing. Oh deary me.'

Ren closed her eyes: 'I want to lie down.' Her mother

helped her upstairs and she lay on the bed, her face throbbing.

* * *

'Ren?' She heard her name and struggled to open her eyes.

She squinted up at Vetch, trying to move her mouth, but her tongue was too dry to speak.

'I was afraid of this.'

She held out a hand. Vetch took it in his.

'Who did it? The Governor's man?'

He grimaced, squeezing her hand.

'If only I could..'

'I ... don't worry.' Ren mumbled.

He sighed: 'Mother says will you try some broth?'

She nodded and he helped her to sit up, then she tried standing and leant on him as they made their way downstairs. Her head buzzed and banged. She sipped awkwardly from her spoon with her swollen mouth.

'Food and rest. The fastest way to get better,' her mother said, attempting a smile.

The next morning, Ren's mouth was stuffed with thistledown and her eyes with pebbles. Sitting and resting, dozing on and off all day, she couldn't think about anything. Vetch decided that Ren should speak to Captain Pallet, while her face still showed the evidence of Grist's maltreatment. Ren didn't want to go up to the Barrow Hall again, so Vetch had a word with Master Greenweed.

By the third day, the swelling had reduced, although her skin was yellow and purple, and one eye black and bloodshot. Count Saffron, as the Court Examiner, came to visit with

Captain Pallet, Head of the Barrow Guards, accompanying him.

Ren's mother fretted she had nothing prepared to offer Saffron as a refreshment.

He begged her not to worry, insisting all he required was a few quiet moments with Ren.

She repeated the whole episode with Grist, and Pallet made notes, examined her face and asked questions. Ren explained that she'd had headaches, dizziness and slight confusion, but she was recovering.

'But I do feel anxious, my Lords.' She began, then stopped.

They waited for her to carry on.

'I don't want to come to the Barrow Hall, if Grist - I mean what if he - ?'

A flicker of anger crossed Saffron's face, he looked across at Pallet.

'Captain Pallet will speak to Grist - you need to be able to go about your work without fear of a beating.'

Ren blushed. 'My Lady Lilac has dismissed me from her service.'

Saffron gave her a questioning look.

'My Lord. I, I told her I was going to witness against her.'

'Ah, yes of course.'

He stood up and gathered his coat around him. 'I think our visit has been useful.'

Captain Pallet agreed, and added: 'I'll ensure that Grist won't bother you again.'

'When will I be called to give evidence?'

'The hearing is set to begin in four days time. A message

will be sent.' Saffron gave a slight bow, and they left.

Ren spent the next couple of days sitting on the front step, eyes closed, letting the sun warm her face, listening to the hum of bees, the distant sigh of the surf, the everyday chatter of neighbours as they passed. Although she relaxed back into herself, no longer feeling like cloth on tenterhooks being stretched tight, she couldn't stop herself wondering about Bark, trying to imagine his home in Samara. She'd never seen a palace or a castle, though she'd heard tales, rich and exotic, and when she remembered how she'd treated him, she blushed - a king's son. Thinking about it, she decided he wasn't that different to other men. Despite her anger towards him, she ached for his touch, his lips, his smell, certain she'd never see him again.

She went over every decision she'd made in the last few weeks. She mulled over the discussions and arguments, wanting so much to justify herself. She talked to her mother and Vetch, questioning them and herself during their meals.

'Have I done the right thing?' she fretted.

'Be honest with your evidence, let the court decide what's right,' her mother reasoned.

'I'll have to speak about Lilac, in front of nobles!' She felt faint at the thought. 'Sometimes right and wrong don't seem clear in my mind.'

'You've just got to remember whose side you're on,' Vetch said. 'It's simple.'

But was it? She could see Grist enjoyed hurting people, yet she saw he had his reasons. And Lilac? Bark? They were educated, more knowledgeable than her. They said they wanted to do good, even if Ren didn't understand or agree with their methods. She felt instinctively it was right to have saved Bark's life from the 'gettory. Was any cause worth a human life, she wondered?

On the third afternoon, as she hummed and tied bean poles together, she glimpsed a hooded figure on the far side of the allotment, crouched beside her bucket. The figure looked up, saw Ren and disappeared through the hedge. She waited, but he didn't come back, so she went to investigate. A piece of paper stuck out from under her bucket. It read:

> *Come Tonight and Witness what we have achieved with the Azurro.*
> *Before you give Evidence to the Barrow Court, hear our own, Please.*
> *I rely on your Good Heart, Bark*
> *Meet behind the Shebble Inn, Tonight,* 8 *o'clock*

Whoever left the message would be far away now. She'd go. It might be her last chance to see him.

After the evening meal of soup and bread, she said she needed some sea air. Her mother gave her a sidelong glance.

Vetch said: 'You're not worried about tomorrow?'

She shook her head.

'Good. I'm off to a meeting tonight, over the west of town. I may be late.' And he'd gone.

Taking a cloak, Ren stepped out into the warm May evening. The walls of the town glowed apricot, leaves flashed silver, the air smelled of the sea. Alert for strangers, she walked the lanes near the Dyeing Sheds, looking around to be sure she wasn't being spied on, then turned a corner into the alley, behind the Inn. It was deserted. Without a sound, the masked Alchemist appeared at her side:

'I'm afraid I must blindfold you.' He took a scarf and tied it round her eyes.

She felt the fabric of his sleeve as he led her. She couldn't tell which direction.

'Careful now, there are steps.'

The steps were steep, then she heard their footsteps echo in a tunnel. Coming out, it was dank, smelling of seaweed, the sound of sea breaking below on one side, echoing back off stone walls on the other. Out of the sun now, she pulled her cloak closer. The Alchemist led her to a door. She heard a key turn and they entered a cramped corridor. Once he'd shut and locked the door again, he removed her blindfold. He took a lit candle from a niche in the wall and she blinked, adjusting to the gloom. The sharp stench of the dye stuffs took her breath away; the corridor opened out into a large basement workshop, high and wide. She looked around at the machinery and tools of a Dyer: large vats of liquid sitting on fires, racks for holding material, big wooden stirrers stained all colours.

'Ren!'

She heard that familiar voice that set her insides jumping:

'Bark?'

He stepped into the light. She wanted to embrace him, but held back. He came to her, with concern:

'How are your wounds?' He touched her cheek lightly, she flinched.

'Better.'

'They've not marred your beauty.' He smiled.

It only occurred to her later to wonder how he knew. She looked around. The Alchemist had disappeared.

'Why did you contact me?'

'I want you to see the process.' Bark took her hand, she withdrew it.

'Please?'

She followed him to one large vat. He pointed: 'We ferment the leaves of Azurro here.'

She looked down into a murky yellow stew:

'You don't need to grind the plants in preparation?'

'No, no. Much easier - we just leave them to soak.' He took her to the next vat.

'Then here, within a couple of days, we stir the liquid: Azurro pulp sinks to the bottom and we dry it to a paste.' He showed her a jug of muddy paste.

'Now!' He took her to a steaming vat, the stench so strong she put a hand to her face. With wooden tongs, Bark lifted a hank of material clear of the liquid.

'But it's yellow!' Ren exclaimed.

'Wait.'

There, before her eyes, the fabric turned from yellow, to green and finally to a deep blue.

'The air finishes the process!'

He dropped the fabric into another tub of water, ready for rinsing.

'And you've done all this since I last saw you?' Ren could hardly believe it.

He stirred the fabric in the water with the tongs, releasing a whirl of blue.

She watched him pushing at the material.

'We can dye it any number of times and get a richer colour too.'

Ren wandered, looking back over the vats: 'How many of you?'

'Just two of us. No Grinders. No Shebblers either.' He smiled.

She persisted: 'Is the dye caustic, or poisonous?'

'No, and there's no shell dust to clog up the lungs.'

She leant over the edge of the vat staring into the bubbling hot liquid, remembering her own days in the Dye Sheds: the friendships, the singing, the sense of community.

He examined her face: 'Have I convinced you?'

'You've convinced me how dangerous this dye is for the Gild on Calico.'

She pointed to the vats: 'If there's no need to collect shells, then there's no need for Shebblers. Or Grinders - nothing to grind. What will all those men do?'

'Oh Ren, don't just think about the problems.'

She shook her head: 'It's easy for you to say that. The Overlord's son with a country full of Azurro. I've my family - *all* the families of the Blue Hands - to consider. I have to think about their welfare.'

Bark sighed: 'You must confess how quick the process is compared to Shebble dye.'

Reluctantly, she nodded.

'You have to imagine a different future, one that you've created, not one forced on you by a changing world beyond your shores. And look.' He took her to another room where dried fabric hung from the ceiling. 'Look at the quality of the blue. Samara dye and kersey cloth - a union of east and west.'

She took a piece of fabric and rubbed it between finger and thumb. Even in candlelight she could see its gloss and depth of colour.

'What do you think?' Bark watched her.

The quality of the dye was undoubted, and Ren was torn in two.

'It's - it's all wrong!'

Bark took her in his arms and kissed her. She pushed him away:

'Is this your attempt to sway me?'

'No.' He looked sheepish. 'I just couldn't resist your lips.'

She grew angry: 'Who is this Alchemist? He's acting against all the articles of the Gild.'

He stood silent awhile.

'My father will be interested in obtaining this. See? A new market for Calico dyed cloth.'

'That doesn't help the Shebble workers and Grinders.'

Ren stared at Bark over a great divide - they would never agree.

Out of the shadows stepped the Alchemist.

'The hour's late, I'll escort you back.'

Bark asked her to wait a moment. He returned with a package.

'Will you take this to Lilac?'

'I don't work at the Hall anymore, I told you.'

He paused. 'I ask you to do it, as a favour to me.'

She took it without another word, and turned away, an ache in her heart, bitter that their last conversation should be about Lilac. At the door again, the Alchemist tied the blindfold on. She caught the scent of smoke as he blew out the candle, then they were out in the sea air again. Below, waves were slapping the sea walls, the wind buffeted her.

She stumbled with the package up the steps. He grasped her arm and they followed a long winding route through the streets until he whispered:

'Before you go, take this.' She found a letter placed into her free hand. 'Give it only to Saffron, the Court Examiner. It contains important information.'

'What about? Who are you?'

She removed her blindfold and blinked, about to speak - the Alchemist had gone. She saw the end of her row of cottages, ragged clouds blowing like cloth across the moon. She turned over the letter and package in her hands: she was always in the dark, do this, carry that, but no-one told her why. No more - after the hearing - she'd be free, wouldn't she?

The next morning dawned overcast and blustery. Master Greenweed knocked early:

'You'll be needed tomorrow, to give evidence. You can listen to the whole proceedings if you wish.' He eyed her up and down. 'How quickly you have changed, Ren. Not like a Lady's maid anymore.'

'What's wrong with that?' Vetch demanded.

She blushed: 'I'll go back to the Hall so I can make myself ready.'

She'd have to face Lilac, give her the parcel from Bark and she mustn't forget the letter for Saffron. Kissing her mother, she couldn't help a few tears. It reminded her of her first visit to the Hall with Greenweed - how long ago that seemed. She could hardly remember the young woman she'd been, although she remembered the nerves. Her mother wiped Ren's face with her apron.

'There, there. It'll be over soon.'

'That's what I'm afraid of.'

She hugged Vetch, who told her: 'What you do is right, your heart tells you.'

As she stepped out the door, the wind caught her cloak and she put a hand to her hair. She needed her coif, tucked in her pocket, waiting for her transformation back into a maid at the Barrow Hall.

'What news?' She asked Greenweed, as they walked side by side.

'The rumours fly about, no-one knows what to believe.' He shook his head. 'Everyone knows you're to give evidence against the Lady Lilac.'

She moaned, sick at the thought, having to face people, the centre of gossip.

'What do you think will happen? To me, I mean.'

He looked up with faraway eyes.

'I don't know, Ren. We shall just have to wait and see.'

Chapter 11
Vetch

Ren slipped through the Hall, keeping her head down to avoid people and conversation, aware they were staring. She shut her door and leaned back against it. Was this really hers, her place in the Barrow Hall? Everything seemed different, alien. Had she ever really belonged? She filled a bowl with cold water and rubbed her face and neck with a cloth. She found a pink skirt and bodice, a clean chemise, and dressed thoughtfully. She must act the part, she told herself and gave her hair a thorough brush before she tied it up tight, pinning the coif in place. Grasping the package, she made her way to Lilac's room.

Taking a deep breath, she was about to knock when the Guard outside stopped her:

'What's that?'

'Oh, a scarf, from my mother.'

He grunted assent and Ren knocked. A young maid opened the door.

It was Nutmeg, the skinny kitchen girl who'd brought her chamomile the day she'd had sun fever.

'Ren! What are you doin 'ere?' she whispered.

'I've got a parcel. Give it to Lilac,' she whispered back, thrusting it into her hands

'Who are you talking to?' Ren heard Lilac call.

'Wait!' Nutmeg thrust the package back and shut the door.

There were voices, then she opened it again.

'You're to come in and I'm to fetch you mugs o' tea.'

Ren's heart sank, she didn't want to face Lilac. She clasped the package tight. Nutmeg did an awkward curtsey:

'Ren, your Ladyship,' and scurried off.

They stood looking at each other. Lilac broke the silence.

'You have something for me?'

Ren held out the package: 'From Bark.'

Lilac flushed: 'You've seen him?'

Ren nodded.

'What news?' Lilac asked.

'I think the parcel holds material.'

Lilac, her cheeks pink, asked in hushed tones: 'Is he safe?'

Ren nodded. After a pause Lilac said:

'And you are well?'

'I was beaten by Grist.'

'Oh.' Lilac's eyebrows raised. 'I'm sorry…'

Silence stretched.

The kitchen girl returned: 'Tea's up.'

'No, Nutmeg!' Lilac reproved her. 'Remember what I told you.'

'Oops, sorry your Ladyship. I keep forgetting.'

Lilac smiled and the atmosphere softened.

Ren blurted: 'Tomorrow. At the court.'

Lilac put a hand up: 'Do what you must.'

Ren left without drinking her tea.

She ate her evening meal down with the maids and servants, as she'd done in her months of training. In a low room off the kitchen, they sat at a long refectory table on benches. Ren looked around at the eyes showing puzzlement and mistrust.

'Do you still work here?' A maid frowned.

'Did she ever?' Another servant addressed the table and jerked a thumb Ren's way.

What could she say? She felt as confused and unsure as they were.

'I'm here at the Court Examiner's request. To give evidence.'

The maids all tutted and whispered. One said to Ren:

'She's strange, your Lady.'

'She's not my Lady. She's dismissed me.'

'Deserves all she gets, that Lilac. Up to all sorts, I've heard.' The servant put a finger to his nose in a knowing way. 'Think's she's so high and mighty.'

'Mistress of the Revels!'

'Whoever heard the like?'

'Consorting with smugglers' 'And spies!'

It was as if a fizzy wine had been unstoppered, the room erupted with gossip and speculation, criticising Lilac's odd ways. Ren found herself wanting to defend her, despite herself. Lilac *was* different, she chose a path of her own. Deep down, she admired Lilac's independent spirit, her refusal to bow to customs and expectations. She fumed at their narrow, ignorant comments and retired to her room as soon as she could, wondering what they were now saying about her.

She woke early and looked at the wood above her. She

was in her box bed. She ran her hand over the wooden frame, reluctant to start the day. A sinking feeling swamped her and she sighed. Was it barely four months since she came to the Hall with her red and green serpentine stone and the spelling book? How childish these items seemed to her now - pointless memories of home and girlhood, their charms couldn't help her now. There were no duties to perform for Lilac, more time to do nothing but wait until she was summoned to give evidence.

She wondered where Bark was - she'd done as he'd asked and delivered the parcel. She remembered the letter the Alchemist had given her - who was this strange man, and why was the letter important? Who else was a Mazard? There was no-one to talk to, to ask for advice. She'd just have to say what she knew and felt in her heart to be right. It would all be out in the open in a few hours. At that thought she buried her head in the covers, and groaned.

She rose, washed and dressed with care, brushing her hair and twisting it round her head, pinning her coif in place, remembering Lady Rose's lessons. If you want people to take you seriously, a sober outward appearance reflects a well-ordered reliable nature. She could hear her saying it. Would Lady Rose be at the hearing, and what would she think of her when the full evidence came out?

She sighed; for all her attempts to be calm and ordered, she didn't feel it inside. Her hands trembled, she couldn't sit still, her body restless. She went to the kitchen, grabbed an apple and climbed up to the Lookout Tower; at least she could breathe fresh air and have a view. The wind blew from the north. The pennant on the flag pole snapped, the sea wore ruffles of white. She shivered a little as she bit into her apple, wrinkled but sweet, from the previous autumn's crop, kept in the dark cellars of the Hall. If they were stored carelessly they bruised and rotted. Only the Hall had space for an apple store; at home, apples were crushed to make bubbly liquor or preserved in jams and pickles.

Ren leant on the parapet thinking about helping her mother with the making of pickle, eyes wandering over the scene below. Near the Grinding Sheds she saw a crowd gathering, one or two folk waving to a cart as it wheeled to the doors, a man running. Even from this far away, she sensed alarm in their movements. It made the hairs on her neck stand on end. A gull flew overhead, keening. It was the shed where Vetch worked! With a terrible sense of foreboding, she scrambled down the stairwell. She flew along the corridor, her heart pumping. She raced down the main staircase to the great front doors. The Guards glanced at her. She scanned the street - nothing. She hurried down the servants' stairs and threw open the kitchen door.

All the staff were silent, looking at her, frozen in the middle of cooking. The pots hissed and the fire crackled. Then she saw Moss, twisting her hands, staring with wide eyes:

'Ren,' she said. 'There's bin an accident.'

Ren and Moss charged through the streets, pushing past the market stalls.

Moss pulled her toward the Spittal House, calling over her shoulder:

'Your mother's on her way.'

Off the market square stood a white stone building - a knife, a leaf and a bowl were pictured above the front doors. A small knot of workers stood there:

'Here she is!' one called. 'Hurry lass,' said another as the group parted to let them through.

Inside it smelt of herbs, and decaying bodies. Grey walls with high windows let in stripes of sunlight. Narrow beds lined the room: Ren hurried down looking left and right: past thin silent women; wailing children; old men coughing blue stuff into buckets. A doctor was bending over Vetch. As she approached, the doctor drew up a sheet to cover him so she could only see his face.

Vetch moaned, his brow shiny with blue powder and sweat. Her mother arrived breathless, her eyes full as she grabbed the doctor's arm: 'How is he?'

Moss whispered to Ren: 'He has to lose his right hand.'

Fern knelt beside him: 'Hold on my brave boy.' She stroked his hair.

The doctor turned to Ren:

'We can use you, if you're willing?'

Ren paled: 'What must I do?'

'Talk to him. Take his mind away from our task.'

A woman in a bloody apron bent to Vetch with a bottle of cloudy liquid:

'Here, take a few mouthfuls, lad.'

His mother cradled his head while the nurse tilted the bottle to his lips. He sipped, coughed.

'A few more mouthfuls.' She held the bottle to his lips

again. He drank and coughed.

'Potation,' Moss whispered again. 'It'll numb the pain.'

'Right, bring him through,' the doctor ordered.

They carried Vetch as gently as they could into a bare room with a marble slab and sluice gutters along the walls. Buckets of water waited beside a table covered in clamps, knives and bandages. In the corner, a brazier was burning, on it a pot of tarry liquid bubbled. The smell caught the back of Ren's throat. Her legs threatened to give way.

Vetch cried out as they laid him on the slab. The doctor pulled down the sheet and Ren saw his right forearm was bent with a jagged bone piercing the bloody flesh, his hand a pink crab split open. He whimpered as the nurse cut off his shirt and tied a leather strip round his upper arm, tightening it with many twists of a wooden stick.

'Another sip for pity's sake,' he pleaded. Moss took the bottle, and poured a few drops into his mouth. His eyes flew open at the chink of metal instruments being prepared. The terror in his face forced Ren forward. She folded his left hand into her breast and held it tight:

'I'm here. Don't be afraid.'

The nurse gave her a pitted wooden slat: 'Make sure his tongue's out the way.'

Ren nodded and pushed it against his mouth. His teeth came down like a vice, a dark glint in his eyes. Moss grasped both Vetch's legs.

'Right?'

The doctor began to saw.

The grinding of metal on bone ripped the air. Vetch

squealed like a pig at slaughter. The rending and splitting set Ren's teeth on edge, her stomach clenched. She gabbled words, to drown out the terrible sound, ignoring the blood and water that splattered at her knees. His hand gripped hers, crushing it. There was a stink of burning flesh. Vetch let out a scream, and fainted.

'Done,' said the nurse,

'Thank you, my dear,' said the doctor.

The nurse bound Vetch's right arm with bandages: 'Now we wait. See how it heals.'

Moss smiled at Ren: 'I've seen men recover from this sort of accident before. It's in nature's hands now.'

Ren looked at her face, scarred with Shebble Pox. Moss was so calm, so dependable, she thought, even in such terrible circumstances. She felt a deep admiration and gratitude.

'Thank you Moss, I couldn't have stood it without you.'

They carried Vetch back to the wooden bed in the main room. Her mother looked down, cheeks wet:

'What have they done to him?' She bent and kissed his unconscious face, then she held Ren tight and Ren gave in to the tears she'd been holding back. After a while she pulled away and looked at her mother's face:

'At least he's alive.'

Moss embraced them both:

'I'll call again to see how he's getting on. He's strong. Have hope.'

Later that evening, Fern and Ren sat round Vetch's bed in a small pool of light, as he spoke about the accident:

'It was the first crude crushing. I'd poured in the Shebble shells and set the grindstone working -' he winced and took a breath '- I saw a rogue shell, and leaned in.. to pick it out. Everyone does it.' He screwed his eyes at the memory. 'This time.. the grindstone,' his voice went smaller, higher, 'it rolled over - pulled my arm.' He began to cry. 'It took two men to reverse it-' he paused. 'I'll never work again. No master'll employ me. No woman will look at me.' He sobbed harder. 'This is the end, my life is over.'

Ren stared at him, she'd never seen her brother cry. She searched to find comforting words.

'No, no Vetch. You'll get well.'

'There's no reason to get well.'

His mother leaned close:

'A man's life isn't over till he takes his last breath. You've many years left, Vetch. No-one knows what's in store. But you have your eyes, your brains. You've a voice. That's why you're a Gild leader. You'll find a good woman, there'll be children - so many joys in this world. Don't turn your back on it. Do it for the memory of your father.'

She took a deep breath - Vetch had drifted off to sleep again.

Ren and her mother sat on, napping for brief periods, only to waken with a start and test Vetch's forehead for fever.

As early light filtered through the windows, Ren woke. She shivered and yawned, her mother beside her, head back against the wall, snoring. Vetch was deep in sleep, two red spots of colour on his cheeks. Rising, she stretched, easing her stiff legs, twisting her head to loosen the tension in her neck. She'd always known the dangers Blue Hands faced; it shook her to see the reality.

She stood at the entrance to the Spittal, watching dawn spread pink over the town. She wandered out, thinking about long-held beliefs, the views of the Blue Hands so deeply ingrained. She'd always taken them to be natural, unquestionable. Now, as the light grew in the east, her thoughts shifted like a light growing inside her. She dared to wonder: what if the world of work didn't involve the dangers of Shebble shell collecting, the difficulties of grinding, of running the risk of Blue Lung from the powder of shells saturating the air in the Sheds?

What if Azurro *could* be incorporated into the Gild? If it was safer, easier and made an equal if not superior dye? Her grandfather would never have suffered Blue Lung, and Kale would have a lifetime ahead of him; her father would be alive, Vetch wouldn't be lying maimed, facing death if his arm didn't heal.

She looked up at the sky shining over her: perhaps Azurro didn't have to mean loss of work for the Blue Hands. It could mean new skills, different jobs. If only the Gild would allow it.

But the rules were strict. That's why The Mazards acted with such secrecy; why Lilac was facing a court hearing; why Ren was going to give evidence condemning her.

She leant on the sea wall and looked out over to the eastern horizon. What about Samara and Bark - the dye would have

156

to be bought, traded from abroad. Could Azurro grow on Calico? No, she doubted the weather conditions were right, and anyway, the Island was tiny, it couldn't grow enough. So how would importing Azurro affect the price of the dye and the profitability of dyeing material? Maybe that's why Braymer and Samara and Calico needed to work together. That's why Charlatan, Bark and Lilac were founder members of the Mazards. Because it would take mutual agreements to maintain their monopoly on blue dyed cloth. And she'd refused to see the possibilities. What a fool, too young and stubborn to understand what had been going on!

She should have trusted Lilac, seen that she was honest and really did mean what she said about helping the Blue Hands. Everything she'd believed had been turned on its head.

And Bark, oh, she'd been so angry with him, she'd let her feelings get in the way instead of listening. She should have asked more questions, tried to see his point of view. She wrapped her arms about herself, shivering, and realised she'd lost her chance. She'd pushed him away! Her heart ached at the thought - would she ever be able to hold him close and say sorry?

'Ren?' A voice broke her thoughts. She saw Master Greenweed hurrying towards her through the market, opening up for the morning.

She threw herself into his arms.

He embraced her: 'How is he?'

'He's survived the night. That's something.'

'I'll visit him later. But first I came to fetch you, for the hearing.'

Ren put a hand over her mouth. 'I forgot all about it. I've missed the first day!'

He waved a hand: 'Don't worry, they postponed it. Have you breakfasted?'

They found a stall with a pot boiling on a fire, a small clay oven, hot with the smell of new loaves baking. Greenweed bought them two mugs of green tea and plump brown rolls of spelt and apricots. They sat on a low wall overlooking the harbour, as the sun warmed up the stones.

'Will you manage today?' he asked. 'I might be able to arrange another postponement.'

Ren blew on her steaming mug:

'No. I've waited long enough. I want this to be over.'

Greenweed shook his head: 'I think it may be just the beginning.'

She took a sip; heat seeped through her, right to her fingertips and toes. She chewed the roll, enjoying the apricot. She'd made up her mind what she was going to say.

Chapter 12
The Devil's Dye

Watching the people filling the Great Hall for the the hearing, Ren remembered Lady Rose had impressed on her that everyone had a colour. At the Hall, Ladies' maids wore shades of pink. Slate grey was for servants who waited on noblemen, but didn't do kitchen work. Kitchen staff, men and women, wore brown calico. Guard uniforms were blue jerkins. Sage green was for Notaries. Only nobles wore Shebble-dyed purple, indigo and black. Turning round, she saw at the back some elder Mistresses and Masters from the Gild in their undyed brown, grey or stone. Colour, Rose said, told you a person's rank before you met them, so you knew how to address them. Now, as people sat in their hierarchies of colour, her pink stood out, she was the only maid sitting there.

On the raised dais were five chairs at a black cloth-covered table and a Notary to record the evidence. A rustling hush and a low murmur of voices filled the Hall as The Council of Five arrived: The Governor wearing indigo, the Court Examiner Saffron in purple, Pan the Harbourmaster in a black cape, Greenweed in a dark green jerkin, wearing his chain of office, and finally, Head of the Barrow Guard, Captain Pallet in a blue doublet and cape edged with maroon.

They seated themselves on the dais. All around the room

were Barrow Guards, standing to attention. Ren noticed Grist slip into a chair below the dais, pulling it back into shadow; she felt sick and was clenching her hands to stop them shaking. She counted to ten, eased her shoulders and loosened her grip, stretching her fingers. Two Barrow Hall servants stood waving great fans to create a breeze, and stir the sluggish air; a maid stood beside jugs of water, set on a table.

In the empty space at the centre of the Hall a servant placed a chair for those who were to be questioned. There was muttering and shifting when Lady Lilac arrived, stiff and unsmiling, accompanied by two Guards. The Notary on the dais tapped a little wooden spindle and called:

'The hearing has now begun.'

The Governor rose to speak formalities:

'I welcome all here today. May I remind everyone of the obligation to be full and truthful in evidence-giving, according to the Law of the Barrow. Truth and Justice go hand in hand.'

'Truth and Justice,' came the reply, then all shook hands with their neighbours in the time-honoured tradition.

The Governor sat and Saffron rose. Ren watched him, his hair greying at the temple, a wiry man, wearing his authority lightly:

'The hearing has been established to decide on the following issues: One, to investigate the nature of the plant discovered in the hands of the person known as Bark, absent and unknown as to his whereabouts today. The importation of this plant contravenes Article 5 of the Gild Regulations.' He held the plant up and people strained to get a glimpse.

160

How ordinary and harmless it looked, Ren thought.

'Two, to determine the exact purpose of the foreign Chapbook,' he waved it as evidence, 'lately found in Lady Lilac's possession, seated over here.' He pointed.

'Three, to discover the involvement of these individuals, including Charlatan of Braymer, also absent, in a secret organisation formed to carry out these activities. Based on our findings, if any are found guilty, this may lead to punishments as set down in the Gild's Articles and Island Regulations. We have witnesses and the accused to question. All those who wish to speak should do so through me and keep good order. Our Notary will keep a record. Thank you.'

He glanced down at his papers, then looked round the room. Ren heard her name called.

A hot blush rose up her neck and cheeks and, for a moment, she thought she was going to faint. Her legs flimsy as paper, she walked to the witness's chair, breathing deeply, keeping her eyes to the floor. Saffron spoke the formal phrase:

'From Truth comes Justice.'

She repeated it clearly, without a tremble. She kept her eyes on Saffron, aware of many other eyes on her.

He looked up and said:

'First, I'd like to express the Court's concern for your brother. We wish him a full recovery.'

'Thank you, my Lord.'

'Now. Explain your position in the Hall to the hearing, if you please.'

Ren cleared her throat and began, explaining her training

as Lady's maid and how she became Lady Lilac's servant.

'And what duties do you perform for her?' Saffron asked.

'All that are usual, my Lord. Waiting on her, helping her with her wardrobe,' she hesitated, ' - running errands.'

'Did she ask you to do anything else, anything unusual?'

Ren took a deep breath: 'Yes, my Lord.' A drop of sweat trickled under her arms.

'Can you tell the hearing what exactly?'

'She asked me to take messages.'

'The Lady Lilac is Mistress of the Revels, is she not?'

'Yes, my Lord.'

'Were these messages to do with revels and entertainments?'

'No, my Lord.'

'Go on.'

'She asked me to join the Mazards.'

'And who are they?'

'A secret society. She made me vow to keep silent.' Ren bent her head.

A brief murmur rose and fell to silence as Saffron said:

'The court requires you to give evidence of what you know. Can you name the members?'

'Bark, Charlatan and my Lady Lilac.'

'Any others?'

'I believe so.'

'Tell us more about the Mazards.'

'She, I mean my Lady, told me that the Mazards were people who wanted to change the world.' Ripples of laughter and disbelief ran around the room. 'To improve the working conditions for the Blue Hands. And.'

'And?'

'To create a new blue dye.'

Many gasped and a louder murmur swelled. Ren stole a look at Lilac, who had her head forward, her eyes on her lap. Saffron raised a hand for silence:

'How do you know this wasn't just fantasy, a wild imagination at work?'

'My Lord, they talked of a new plant from abroad that made the dye and I saw a box of it.'

'Who imported it?'

'The man called Bark, who arrived on The Starfish with Charlatan and the travelling theatre.'

'Where is the man Bark?

She cleared her throat: 'I don't know, sir.' It wasn't exactly a lie.

'What did they call this plant?'

'Azurro.'

'The Devil's Dye! It's the Devil's Dye.' The Governor stood, purple-cheeked, his spittle-flecked lips and eyes wide: 'She is responsible!'

All eyes turned following his outstretched finger, pointing at Lilac. A buzz filled the room - the word was repeated and passed around - Azurro? the Devil's Dye!? People were beginning to talk openly. The Governor continued to shout:

'My own daughter has been plotting against the Isles ever since she returned from Braymer!'

Saffron put up both hands: 'My Lord Governor, calm yourself. Quiet please, nobles and ladies.'

Lilac looked pale; Ren saw Lord Saffron and Captain Pallet

put their heads together. Her heart beat hard, her palms were damp and she rubbed them down her skirt. Looking around she met Grist's narrowed eyes. He scowled at her. She turned away quickly, wondering if her questioning had ended. The room grew quieter but the Governor remained on his feet, determined to speak:

'This dye is a danger!'

'Sire.'

'One drop can blind a man! It burns holes in the worsted and ruins fine silk.'

Saffron raised his voice:

'Governor, I must ask you to desist. You will have an opportunity to speak later. We are in the middle of hearing this young woman's evidence.'

Still muttering, the Governor sat down. Saffron pulled his robe, mopped his brow with a kerchief and eased his shoulders. He began again:

'Now, Ren, what do you know of this Azurro?'

'My Lord, it grows in great abundance in Samara, and it's easy to harvest.'

'How do you know this?

'I read it in a book Travels of a Calico Captain.' There was laughter in the Hall.

'That? It's just a fanciful tale of an old seaman!'

'No, no my Lord. Bark confirmed it. He says Azurro grows as widely as grass. He says it makes a better dye. It's the truth... he knows - he comes from Samara.'

Ren caught Lilac looking up and there were whispers around the Hall.

'And what were the Mazards planning to do with this Azurro?'

'To test it as a dye.'

'Presumably they didn't achieve their aim before they were arrested?'

Ren hesitated then took a deep breath: 'No sire. But Bark escaped - and has since turned the Azurro into dye with the aid of an Alchemist, another Mazard I believe.'

This took everyone by surprise. Grist sat forward. The Governor leapt to his feet again:

'This is wicked and dangerous! Who would *dare* do such a thing?'

Ren noticed Master Greenweed was looking straight into her eyes. She looked away as Saffron spoke again:

'How do you know this?'

Ren blushed and stumbled over her words, her cheeks burned:

'My Lord, I was taken to a dye shop where the process was demonstrated to me.'

'Where? By whom?'

'The Alchemist. He blindfolded me.'

'Why would he do that?'

'So I couldn't see where I was.'

'I mean, why take you to see a demonstration?'

'Because I was going to give evidence. They wanted me to report it. The work took a week. It made a very fine blue.'

The Governor, indignant, called out:

'You trust the word of a maid?'

Ren appealed to the Hall:

'I was a Blue Hand until my 15th year. I know an inferior dye and I know a good mix when I see one. Why, I can tell from a look, the feel, the smell of it.' She saw Lady Rose in the crowd, watching and fanning herself.

'Who was this Alchemist?'

The court went utterly silent, Ren held her head up:

'My Lord, he wore a mask. I never saw his face.'

The Governor burst out again: 'She's confirmed what our spies have been suspecting. Let's get a move on and question the real criminals!'

Saffron clamped his jaw and paused a moment before he spoke:

'I have one more question. Ren, I came to visit you a week past. You sustained some injuries to your face. Will you explain how you received them?'

'The Governor's man Grist accosted me in the street with an arrest warrant. He hit me, and I fell.'

There were tuts and people turned to look at Grist.

'You may return to your seat, Ren.'

The Governor, looking irritable, sat back and crossed his arms. Many courtiers were fanning themselves and whispering. As Ren returned to her seat, she put her hand in her pocket,

'Oh, my Lord.' She hurried back. 'I nearly forgot. I was given this letter by the Alchemist.'

She hesitated, not sure if this was the time to mention it. Too late, Saffron held out his hand and she handed it over. He opened it, took out some sheets and looked over them quickly. He nodded, and Ren returned to her seat. He placed the sheets under his papers, then carried on:

'I call Grist to give evidence.'

Ren hurried toward the back of the Hall so as not to cross his path, and sat next to Lady Rose, who offered her water. They watched Grist swagger to the witness chair.

'From Truth comes Justice.'

'From Truth comes Justice,' Grist replied, looking around the Hall.

'Tell us your name and position, please.'

'Grist - Island Security.'

'What does that entail?'

'What it sounds like - I keep my eyes and ears open for anything that threatens the safety of the Isles, and I take action when I need to.'

'Who do you answer to?'

Grist looked surprised: 'The Governor.'

'I see.' Saffron raised an eyebrow, and glanced over at Captain Pallet. 'Why were you following Lady Lilac on the day you arrested her?'

'I'd got wind of a plot.'

'Who from?'

'Well now, if I told you that I wouldn't be able to do my job, would I? Let's just say I have some trusted informants.' He smirked.

'So what did you discover when you followed Lady Lilac?'

'We caught Lilac and Bark in the maid's room, with a foreign plant and a Chapbook in their possession, regarding making of dye. So I arrested Bark and Lilac.'

'And the maid?'

'At first I thought she wasn't involved. Later I changed my opinion. I questioned her, in order to discover more.'

'And did you?'

'She told me what she's told the court. I think she was involved with the escape of the prisoner. She didn't tell the court that, did she?'

Ren shifted in her chair, but Saffron was pursuing other questions.

'Does your job involve using techniques designed to force confession when questioning suspects?'

'Yes - that's normal.' Grist frowned: 'I do my job the most effective way.'

'So did Bark reveal any information about this plant before he escaped?'

Grist didn't reply, but Ren watched his mouth twisting.

'What, nothing?' Saffron was dry: 'Despite your persuasion?'

'He's a tough one.'

'And when you hit the maid, did it make her more forthcoming?'

'I didn't get a chance..'

Saffron raised his voice and addressed the Hall:

'That is why inflicting suffering in order to coerce information is not approved by the Calico Council. It endangers life and has no proven use in gaining information. Including, and especially, assaulting young women!'

Saffron folded his arms and stared at Grist. The audience muttered; Ren blushed and put a hand to her face.

'Did the Governor approve your methods?'

Grist didn't answer, but looked toward the Governor, who shifted in his seat. Saffron bent to the Notary:

'He did not answer, put that down.'

'So, let us return to the stalk of a plant you found. And the Chapbook. What did it reveal?'

'We couldn't decipher it.' Grist's neck and ears were red.

'And what do your spies tell you about the masked Alchemist?'

Grist looked down.

'Nothing at all? I see. Thank you for your most informative evidence. You may sit down.'

Grist stood and eyed everyone around the Hall.

'Anyone who thinks dissenters or foreigners aren't a threat are fools. I know things. I see things. I hear your whispered conversations, I know what you're thinking. And I've a good memory. The Dye Wars aren't that long ago. Piss and shells make this country rich..' There was a burst of laughter, quickly stifled. 'I'm not paid to be polite, I'm paid to preserve the law.' He pointed round the room. 'My job keeps you safe so you can hold your court investigations.'

Grist marched off, his body stiff, as the Governor clapped in support, and a few others in the Hall murmured agreement. Saffron looked through his papers, spoke quietly with the Notary, then he said:

'I call Lady Lilac.'

Everyone craned round to watch her make her way to the chair. She walked with calm self-assurance, carrying a bundle. Ren thought her impressive.

'From Truth comes Justice.' Saffron spoke. Lilac

responded, her voice clear in the Hall.

'My Lady Lilac, you have heard the evidence against you. These are serious accusations with important consequences and punishments.' He waved the papers in his hand.

Pan the Harbourmaster nodded vigorously.

Saffron held the papers out towards Lilac: 'What do you say?'

Lilac stood and looked around the Hall:

'Justice Saffron, Governor, Members of the Council and Nobles, I confess to all these accusations.'

The Governor stood and pointed: 'She condemns herself!' He glared around the room challenging anyone to disagree.

'Yes, we heard it too, thank you Governor.' Saffron turned to him. The Governor sat down. Saffron turned back to Lilac: 'Carry on.'

'I wish to be allowed an opportunity to explain myself.'

Saffron turned to the Council members: Master Greenweed and Captain Pallet nodded. The Governor beckoned to Grist, who came over. Pan, the Governor and Grist put their heads together, discussing.

The Governor stood up. 'The evidence is clear. She's guilty. Why listen to justifications?'

Pan agreed: 'We shouldn't be giving a platform to sedition!'

The Hall erupted into anger and dissent. Some shouted: 'We should hear her arguments.' 'Let her speak.' Others roared: 'Rebels have no place here.'

'Hear, hear,' Grist cried.

'Order!' cried Saffron. 'Order.' The voices died down. Saffron spoke loudly: 'I don't need to remind you of our principles: from Truth comes Justice. We must weigh everyone's truth to reach a just decision. I join my vote on The Council of Five to those who say let her speak.'

He turned to Lilac.

'Go ahead.'

The Governor and Pan continued to mutter and shook their heads.

Lilac smiled at Saffron:

'Thank you. This was to be my final argument. Instead I will begin with it. May I ask Ren to come and assist me?'

Ren stood and Saffron beckoned her over. She edged her way through the seats. Lilac opened the parcel; it contained blue cloth. She gave a corner to Ren and said:

'Would you stand over there?'

Ren walked across the Hall and lifted her arm. Lilac raised the other end to display the material - a deep subtle blue that hinted of many colours, yet uniformly dyed to a rich lustrous finish. As it swayed, catching the light, there were murmurs from the Hall.

'The quality speaks for itself.' She looked round the room.

'My Lords, may I?' Justice Saffron came down from the dais to feel the texture and examine the cloth at close hand. Greenweed followed him, smiling. Saffron muttered:

'Amazing, hm.'

'This is why I've taken these risks.' Lilac spoke loudly: 'Why I knowingly acted outside the jurisdiction of the Gild and the Isles of Calico. Because I believe the future of the Island's dye trade lies with this new plant: Azurro.'

The Governor stood and shouted:

'We have a strict monopoly system, agreed between Braymer and Calico. We can't abandon that without Braymer's consent. You'd overthrow our unique Shebble dye for an untried and risky element. It's madness! I say punish them all.'

Saffron went back to his table and bent down to his papers. He fished out the letter Ren had given him, and waved it at the Governor, speaking so all could hear:

'My Lord Governor. I have here further evidence that is pertinent to this hearing.'

The Hall fell silent as all eyes turned to Saffron.

'This is a letter from Master Tawney, of the Merchant Gild of Braymer, addressed to you, sir.'

The colour drained from the Governor's face.

'After a cursory glance it appears to refer to private negotiations regarding the amount of cloth dyed on Calico. Were you too acting outside the jurisdiction of the Gild's Charter?'

The Governor and Pan the Harbourmaster glanced at each other along the table. Saffron finally lost his temper, addressing his remarks to the Hall:

'May I remind you, Governor, that you were elected to the Council to help us order ourselves, to govern society on our behalf, not for your own personal use of power.'

There was a gasp of shock from the assembled people. The Governor said nothing. Saffron carried on:

'We who gave you your duties may also take them away if we judge they are not being carried out responsibly.'

At that moment many people started speaking at once.

The Governor began shouting: 'You fools…!'

Greenweed raised his voice: 'This cloth, might I request..'

The Notary flustered, not knowing what to write, appealed to Saffron who called out:

'Order! Order please!'

But as the voices in the Hall died away, everyone heard a growing tide of noise outside. Loud voices, many voices, shouting as one. At that moment a Guard dashed into the Hall and straight up towards the dais to Captain Pallet. They had a brief conversation, then the Captain stood -

'Court Examiner, I'm needed. The Blue Hands are marching on the Hall.'

Chapter 13
The Blue Hands

Saffron addressed the room: 'I suspend the hearing.'

Captain Pallet marched off, other Guards following him. Ren had forgotten about the Gild's plan with worrying about Vetch and her nerves at the hearing. The chanting outside grew louder. Voices were booming though the great doors; she could hear the words:

'The Blue Hands march, the Blue Hands cry - we defy the Devil's Dye!'

Saffron called loudly so all could hear: 'What is this commotion? Greenweed - Did you authorise it?'

Master Greenweed raised his arms: 'I believe it's a convocation of the Gild - men and women come to make their views known to the Council. It is their right.'

The Governor, who'd recovered his poise, smiled:

'Quite so - they are wise to denounce this dye.'

The nobles and courtiers were standing in groups, discussing what to do. Greenweed helped Ren fold the blue cloth:

'You gave your evidence well.' He smiled. Ren found herself close to tears:

'Vetch should have been out there, leading the Blue Hands.'

Lilac stamped her foot and cried:

'The Blue Hands will spoil everything! Ignorant fools. I'll

go and speak to them.'

Ren stared at Lilac criticising her friends and families. She caught Lilac's arm, insisting:

'No! I'll talk to them.'

'You?' Lilac said with a disbelief that angered her even more. Ren turned on her heel and strode to the Hall doors.

The sun was high, the Blue Hand banners fluttered. The marchers struggled to keep their poles upright. Ren looked out over the streets stretching away down to the market filled with hundreds of men and women, young and old. The marchers had come to a halt at the steps of the Hall. Clouds scudded across the blue, hiding the sun, shadowing faces. Each waved their bandanna, a sea of brightly coloured fish. Some were shaking their fists in the air, their shouts of 'Dye, Dye, The Devil's Dye!' were blown about. She could see anger and fear on their faces. Ren raised her arms, lifted her voice and called:

'Fellow Blue Hands!'

She shouted again, waving her arms to gain attention, over the noise of the crowd:

'Blue Hands, listen!'

Some at the front turned to each other, questioning:

'Who's she?' 'What did she say?'

Someone shouted:

'She's no Blue Hand. Look at her.'

The men took up the chants again:

'Dye, Dye! The Devil's Dye!' 'Shebblers forever.' 'We oppose Azurro!'

'Down with foreigners, enemies of the Gild.'

Ren looked out at this angry mob and thought of Vetch, who'd worked so hard to organise this march, who should have been standing there now, one of the leaders, chanting. But he lay in the Spittal House, brought down by the very thing these people wanted to protect.

She looked round their expectant faces, weather-beaten or young and fresh, all expressing worry and concern; faces she understood. She cupped her hands to her mouth and cried:

'Listen!'

At the back of the crowd were women and girls, who recognised Ren - they were urging quiet.

'Let her speak. She's from a Blue Hand family.'

At the front of the crowd, just below her, Moss cried:

'She's Vetch's sister.'

Ren took her chance:

'Aye. Vetch - true Gildsman, strong and honest, a man who fights for your rights. Today he lies in the Spittal House, injured. The Grinder has taken his means of livelihood.'

A sob rose in her throat, she swallowed it down:

'I may look like a Lady's maid; but once my hands were blue, like yours. Like my mother's. I too fight for your rights. The Gild is our power, it gives status, it safeguards skills. It's our family, it unites us. An honoured tradition stretching back hundreds of years. Our fathers and mothers, grandmothers and forefathers were protected by the Gild. It's ensured the importance of our Shebble dyed cloth over the whole cosmos!'

There were cries of 'Aye!' She paused, took a breath, the

crowd waited.

'But like an old grandfather, the Gild also restricts us, the Charter's rules and articles bind us with ties, keeping us to dangerous old methods. My grandfather had Blue Lung. My father was a Shebbler. We lost him to the sea.'

Women were nodding. An old woman cried out:

'I lost my man to the Shebble shells too.'

Another women shouted: 'That's the true price of the blue dye - a man's life.'

Ren nodded: 'And now my brother Vetch, injured by his work.' The crowd were silent and she raised her voice again:

'There are many lands beyond our Isles, with plants and animals, knowledge and skills that we don't have. Knowledge knows no boundaries: it's coming. Sailing over oceans, crossing great plains. The cosmos is changing whether we want it to or not.

'Azurro is superior to Shebble blue. It's safer. I urge you - we can learn the mystery of Azurro. Incorporate it into our Gild. Be at the forefront of the dye trade, not left behind by old practices. Look outward, form alliances and create new opportunities.' She saw Bark beaming up at her from the crowd and lost concentration. He cheered:

'Well said!'

Men turned round to see who had spoken. Voices shouted:

'Who's he?' 'A foreigner!' 'A spy?'

'Blue Hands!' She drew attention back to herself: 'I want to protect your skills and livelihood. Banning Azurro won't save you. Embrace change, take control of the future. Save our dye industry!'

A woman called out:

'What should we do?'

'Aye - how are we to get this Azurro?' another woman called. An old man roared:

'Ye cannot change the Gild rules just like that!'

Moss lifted her voice: 'We should discuss this with our Gild!'

Ren cried: 'Go back to your Gild. Hold meetings; talk with the Masters and Mistresses.'

Master Greenweed slipped in beside her and smiled. Behind him on the steps of the Great Hall were Saffron, Lilac and other nobles; the Governor had disappeared. She blushed red:

'Master Greenweed. Forgive me if I have spoken out of turn.'

'Not at all. You've made my job easier.'

She stepped back as Greenweed spoke out:

'I have a confession to make!'

The crowd went still, as all strained to hear what the Master would say.

'I, Master of the Gild, am also the Alchemist who has worked in secret to produce dye with Azurro.'

Ren gasped. Confusion began to swell. Greenweed turned to Lilac, who came forward holding the cloth. Between them they held it aloft so the sun shone on it and all could see its bright blue colour, dancing in the wind.

Someone yelled:

'That's Shebble dyed!' 'Aye, how do we know?'

Greenweed raised his voice: 'I swear to you it is Azurro dyed.'

Others shouted: 'Look at it shine.' 'What a finish.' People

were pushing and crowding forward to get a closer look at the fabric. The crowd shifted as groups began to discuss and argue with each other. Then a new voice rang out:

'Would you listen to a Gildmaster who lies to you?' The Governor stood at the edge of the Hall steps.

'I have done this to protect the future of the Gild, not undermine it,' Greenweed cried out.

The Governor sneered, appealing to the masses:

'He disregards the rules and regulations he's supposed to uphold. He doesn't respect you!'

Greenweed countered, desperate to sway the mood:

'I had to act secretly. Now I'm sure of Azurro. I believe the Gild should adapt its articles. Incorporate this new dye into our work practices.'

The crowd looked from one to the other, uncertain and growing impatient.

The Governor spoke confidently:

'*Must* adapt to Azurro? He makes it sound so simple.' Playing the crowd, he raised his voice in anger:

'Do you know where Azurro comes from? Samara! A great country far away, ruled by a savage Overlord. A man who negotiates with swords, not words. Greenweed works in secret with Charlatan from Braymer. And Bark, a spy from Samara! What are they planning?'

The crowd muttered uneasily. The Governor went on:

'It will take a fleet of ships to bring the plant here! That's a costly business. Where will the money come from - out of thin air?'

Some people cried. 'No - out of our pockets!'

Others shouted in agreement.

The Governor called again:

'Our Shebble dye's our own to harvest. The profit's ours. We must protect our industry, not give it away to foreign merchants.'

Some of the crowd cheered: 'Aye!' 'The Governor's right.'

Now other voices rose, 'Wait. We must talk.' 'The Gild must decide. Maybe there's other ways?'

The Governor continued:

'This dye is evil, it'll bring nothing but trouble. Listen to me, your Governor. I say ban Azurro - The Devil's Dye!'

In the midst of the crowd Grist started pushing and shouting:

'Down with the Devil's Dye! Death to the Mazards!'

Ren stood frozen as events spiralled. Moss, near the front, raised her arms, facing the crowd, and called: 'Brothers and sisters - the Gild must talk first!'

'Aye,' a man agreed. Next to him someone shouted: 'No!' and punched the other's face. Immediately, fists were flying; some folk pushed, pulled and ripped shirts, others fought them off.

Ren pleaded with the crowd: 'Stop! Stop!'

No-one took any notice. She saw Grist hitting out, encouraging the fighting. He reached to grab Bark's shirt, swinging a fist. They disappeared from view in a brawl. The wind nearly ripped the blue material out of Lilac's hand as it flew up over the disarray of fighters. Ren turned to appeal to Saffron, but he'd gone. Bundling up the material, Lilac pulled her towards the Great Doors:

'This way.'

'But what about…' Ren turned to the crowds. A stone came flying, just missing her head. She ran for the doors, slipping in, away from the shouting and screaming outside.

Lilac put a hand on Ren's shoulder: 'Thank you.'

Ren flushed, saying nothing.

Greenweed and Saffron were deep in discussion at the back of the Hall. Pan the Harbourmaster and the Governor were nowhere to be seen.

'We'll return to my room until order has been restored and the hearing resumes.' Lilac took her arm: 'Come along.'

Ren pulled her arm away and ran off.

Lilac called: 'Ren. Ren!'

Grasping her skirts, Ren ripped off her cap, letting her hairpins slip out, and raced down the back stairs, through the kitchens and out of a side gate. She saw the crowd, heard the roar of angry voices and headed towards it.

Voices were screaming: 'Down with the Devil's Dye!' Faces were contorted with bared teeth and wild eyes like animals. The crowd had turned into a mindless mob, wielding sticks, throwing stones or vegetables from the stalls. Ducking to avoid arms and missiles, she forged through the crush of people. An elbow caught under her chin and she stumbled. A foot stamped on her ankle. Trapped by the thrashing of legs around her, she grabbed a woman's skirt:

'Help me!' she cried. The woman pulled her up and thrust her face into Ren's:

'See what you've done?'

Before she could think of an answer, the crowd dragged

them apart again. Hobbling on a painful leg and chin aching, jostled and pushed, she searched through the chaos; she caught a glimpse of Bark, between the legs of the crowd and fought hard to reach him. A hand landed on her shoulder. She twisted round and saw Kale with Moss and Tern. Kale frowned:

'Trying to get your head knocked off?'

She gasped: 'I'm looking for Bark.'

Kale let go of her shoulder.

'Please help me.' She grabbed Moss's arm. They were struggling to keep together in amongst the mass of bodies.

Moss shouted: 'Is it the dye or the man you're saving?'

Ren appealed to Kale: 'The crowd'll kill him! Please.'

Kale pulled her: 'Stick with us. C'mon.' Ren limped after Moss as Tern and Kale together forced a way through to Bark, lying on the ground with a bloody forehead, surrounded by men kicking. Tern pulled them off, crying:

'Stop this!'

'Bark?' Ren knelt to him and his eyes flickered open.

'My shoulder,' he murmured.

Moss remonstrated with the young hotheads:

'Calm down. See to your comrades.'

Tern bent and lifted Bark to his feet with Kale the other side. Moss led the way, but the young men formed a barrier, shouting:

'Don't let him get away!'

Kale faced up to them: 'We're taking this man to the Spittal. Out of our way.'

The young men jeered:

'He's a spy. A dirty foreigner.' 'We want him.'

Kale refused to budge: 'Do you want murder on your hands?'

Moss stood firm beside him:

'We need unity, not disarray. One for all and all for one.'

'But he's not one of us.' A red-haired youth pointed an angry finger at Bark.

Moss faced him: 'Hush, Oak. We need to talk, not fight. We'll speak to Brother Vetch, to see what he thinks.'

The lad calmed down and asked:

'How is Vetch?'

The young men dropped their threatening poses, wiping their faces with bandannas, letting them pass.

'Give him our good wishes.'

Moss nodded.

No-one else tried to stop them. The brawling crowds were forced into smaller groups as the Barrow Guards gained control over the situation, and the noise died down.

Ren was hot and and her bruised ankle ached badly by the time they reached the Spittal House; it was cooler in the stone building and they found Vetch asleep watched over by his mother.

'What's this?' Fern asked, looking at Bark's bloody head.

'There's been some disagreement,' Kale said, as he and Tern lowered Bark down to sit on a bed.

'I'll fetch water.' Fern went off.

Ren bent down to her brother: 'Vetch.'

He opened his eyes slowly and took in the group. Bark

leant forward with his one good hand and reached out for Vetch's:

'I'm Bark. I'm sorry to hear of your trouble.'

Vetch wouldn't take his proffered hand, but turned to Ren:

'Why have you brought *him* here?'

'Vetch, listen. Who do you think the Alchemist is?'

Vetch, dazed, blinked at Ren.

'Master Greenweed, the Gildmaster himself!'

He struggled to take it in.

Tern leaned down to Vetch:

'Aye. Right under our noses!'

Ren remembered the night at the Shebble Inn, the Gild meeting and looked from Vetch and Moss to Tern. She could see they were all reconsidering Master Greenweed's advice and actions. He'd fooled them all. No-one spoke.

Fern returned with a bowl and cloth and attended to Bark.

'Don't - he's our enemy!' Vetch cried.

'This man deserves treatment, same as you.'

'My arm..' Bark looked up at Ren.

Kale said: 'I'll fetch the doctor.'

'Ren knows what to do.' Bark smiled up at her.

They watched fascinated as Ren took Bark's limp arm and angled it, then pulled. Bark winced, and held his arm to his chest, saying:

'Ren gave a most remarkable speech in support of Azurro.'

She blushed as he uttered her name. She went deeper red as she felt them all looking at her, especially Kale. Her mother simply mopped Bark's brow.

Vetch frowned:

'So you betrayed our agreement, Ren?'

She spoke up: 'Things have changed. We need to discuss it with you, brother.'

'Yes. We need to be ready..' Tern flushed dark, and trailed off.

Moss said: 'She made everyone think.'

'Aye,' Kale agreed.

Fern left Bark and turned to Ren, touching her bruised chin and tutting. Ren shrugged her off and sat beside Vetch who asked:

'Tell me what you said, Ren.'

'She spoke very highly of you,' said a voice.

They all turned to see a cloaked and hooded figure standing at the foot of Vetch's cot. Lilac removed her hood and smiled down at Vetch, then at Bark.

'What are you doing here?' Ren scowled.

'Ren,' her mother checked her, then she smiled:

'You must be Lady Lilac - welcome.'

Lilac nodded in acknowledgement.

'You put me to shame, Ren. I came to give what aid I can.' Lilac hesitated: 'I - I've never been in the Spittal before.'

'What help can you be?'

There was an awkward silence, until Bark spoke up: 'We all need to talk.'

He looked up at Lilac, then at the others: 'We want the same ends I believe.'

Lilac nodded. Then Vetch spoke so quietly Ren had to lean in to him:

'Will someone tell me what happened.'

Between them, they described the hearing, explained events and discussed what the Council, and the Gild might do next, disagreeing and raising their voices until Fern said:

'That's enough. Vetch needs to rest. And so does this man.'

She patted Bark's shoulder and he winced.

Tern, Kale and Moss stood up to leave; Lilac did too. Ren delayed, in a quandary: should she return with Lilac, or stay here with Vetch, and Bark? She had a room at the Hall, but no official position. Confused, she sat massaging her ankle, resting one elbow on her knee. As if she read her thoughts, her mother said:

'Ren, you should go back with Lilac. I can manage.'

'No. I don't work for her anymore. This is my place now.'

Chapter 14
Moss

Lilac gave an embarrassed laugh as she bent down to Ren: 'Perhaps I was a little hasty.'

Ren flushed red at Lilac trying to make light of the situation. She bit her tongue and bent her head so Lilac wouldn't see her expression. Lilac appealed to the group:

'I tell her to stay indoors, for her own safety, and she rushes off like a vagabond! Every time she goes I am left with the dolt Nutmeg from the kitchen to wait on me. What am I to do with her?' Moss looked down, Tern shuffled his feet and Kale stared at Lilac.

Ren stood up, balancing awkwardly on her good leg, and faced Lilac:

'My Lady, if I have become independent and reckless, acting on my own conscience, you've only yourself to blame. You're the one who made me take secret messages, teaching me to spy and lie. I was following *your* orders. Maybe I've overstepped some line between maid and conspirator, but it's impossible to see where that line lies! Then you dismiss me without thanks or discussion. Now you assume I'll return as if nothing has changed. But everything has changed. Which is why I *insist* you release me from your service and from the Barrow Hall.'

No-one spoke, but only Ren saw Bark smile.

Lilac composed herself and addressed Ren formally:

'You may still be required to give evidence. This is far from over.'

Ren tottered and Moss caught her up:

'There'll be no hearing tonight. Ren can come home with me. She needs rest.'

Lilac looked around the group, bowed her head in acknowledgement and walked away, straight- backed.

Kale, Moss and Tern bade farewell to Vetch. Ren still hesitated until her mother shooed her away.

Ren limped out, holding Moss's arm, into a sunset of crimson and gold. She took a deep breath of the silky air. Water lapped in the harbour, the crowds had dispersed, all was quiet and, for a moment, time stood still. Peace at last.

As she walked up through the twilight, she thought about her position at Barrow Hall and her relationship with her Lady. Ren dug deep into her heart, trying to be truthful: A maid should be neat, honest, biddable, reliable and loyal above all. Lady Rose had drummed that into her. She judged her own actions - was she neat? Sort of. Honest? No! She'd lied to everyone. Biddable? No. Reliable? No, unless you called disappearing for days reliable. And loyal? Ren sighed as she thought about giving evidence against Lilac, the stolen moments with Bark, her meetings with the Gild. And now Ren had just publicly defied Lilac. The only honest thing she'd done was refuse to serve her any more.

She put a hand to the wisps of hair that hung down over her eyes, no longer pinned in place. She should brush it, neaten her appearance, but she didn't care. Tired and worn out, she ached for sleep. Her head hung heavy, her eyes closed, pain shot through her ankle as she stumbled and sank to the ground.

Ren stirred and a woman's hand touched her forehead. She became aware of candlelight flickering. Her leg ached and her head pounded.

'Where am I?'

Moss bent over her:

'You're in my bed. Lilac sent the Hall physician, he diagnosed nervous spirits. And a bad swollen ankle.'

Ren tried to lift herself up on one elbow but sank back with no energy to try again.

'Rest.'

With someone else taking responsibility for her, she let go and found herself racked with sobs. All the anxiety, fear, love and anger of the last months were pouring out. Every time the storm of tears slowed and calmed, another would rise up and she'd sob all over again.

Her chest juddered, her eyes were sore. When she finally emptied out, a weight inside had gone, and she could drift away.

'I'm sorry,' she whispered. Moss took her hand and murmured: 'Sshh.'

She fell into a deep, restful sleep, waking only to sip a herb tea or take a mouthful of bread soaked in milk.

She opened her eyes to see the first rays of sun touch the far wall and heard songbirds outside. She lifted her head and saw Moss sleeping in a chair, covered with a blanket.

'Moss?' she spoke softly. Moss yawned and stretched.

'How long have I been here?'

'Two days and nights.'

Ren sank back, still weak. Moss brought two plates of eggs and bread. Ren ate slowly until every crumb was gone, then lay back in the bed:

'I feel as if I've travelled far away on a long journey. Has the world turned upside down?' Then she remembered: 'Vetch!?'

'He's doing well. Your mother's happy.'

She hesitated then asked: 'And Bark?'

'Talking to Vetch it seems, side by side in the Spittal House. He's persuaded Vetch to speak to the Gild about Azurro.'

Moss sat down again on the edge of the bed, with the plates on her knees, looking into Ren's eyes.

'That man could charm the fish from the sea. I don't trust him. I don't think you should either. I'll wager he has a line a mile long full of hooks with little fishes dangling from each one.'

Ren couldn't meet Moss's gaze.

'He's caught you, hasn't he?'

'He's clever. Different. He's a king's son, but he treats me as if we're the same. Not like Lilac. He really wants to help the Blue Hands.'

'Has he said words of love to you?' Moss looked worried.

Ren blushed: 'So what if he has?'

Moss took the plates away, and came back with a mug of goat's milk for Ren.

'He isn't an Island boy like Kale. He's dangerous, he'll break your heart.'

'You just don't think a man like him would look at a Blue Hand girl like me!'

Moss shook her head: 'Men like him look at Blue Hand girls all the time, then forget them the next day.'

'You're just jealous!'

Moss turned away and touched her blue-speckled face.

'No. I didn't mean that... I'm sorry.'

Moss stood up and took the mug.

'But, but -' Ren stumbled on. 'He's honest about helping the Blue Hands.'

'Is it the Blue Hands he's helping, or himself? See sense. Him and Lilac probably have plans that you don't know about.'

Ren confessed to Moss about the letter from Lilac.

'Oh Ren!'

Ren began to cry, pulling the covers back to get her legs onto the floor. Her bandaged ankle wouldn't hold her.

'Wait Ren. You need more rest and food.'

Her head swam and her muscles trembled, she fell back on the pillows staring at the ceiling:

'As soon as I'm well again -' she sobbed.

'You'll go back to being Lady Lilac's maid. That's the way of things.' She took the mug away.

No no, Ren wanted to shout, you're wrong. She turned her face to the wall.

* * *

After another day's rest, Ren returned to her mother's, who was now caring for Vetch at home. The house was full of Blue Hands coming and going. Moss, Tern and Kale sat in the sun on the front door step discussing events with Vetch and Ren.

'Greenweed offered to step down from his position as Master -.' Kale began.

'To see if the Gild members will support him -.' Moss butted in. Kale carried on:

'He wants a vote to see if he has the Gild's backing to experiment with Azurro.'

'He's not got mine!' Tern was adamant. 'It'll be nothing but ruin for the Shebblers.'

'Vetch and I have already been ruined by the Shebble shell.' Kale plucked a blade of grass, fiddling with it, his eyes on Ren. She couldn't meet his gaze.

'But how will we earn a livelihood?' Tern insisted.

'Oh Tern.' Moss put an arm round his wide shoulders.

'It's alright for you Dyers, they'll still want you.'

Moss hugged him.

Vetch spoke up: 'That's why we need to talk in the Gild. So no-one's put out of work.'

Ren smiled: 'Yes. That's what I've been trying to say.'

Tern stood up: 'You're not a Blue Hand. You've got no vote.'

Ren's smiled vanished. Kale looked across at her:

'I think you talked a lot of sense.'

Tern shook his head: 'She's with the Hall now. It's easy for her to talk.' He strode off.

Vetch cradled his arm, watching Tern go:

'Folk cling to the old ways, but we must persuade Blue Hands. If Azurro is coming, the Gild has got to be part of that.'

Ren said nothing, staring down at her white hands.

It was over a week since the hearing when Lilac came to visit Ren, who took her walking in the allotment so they could speak freely.

'I meant what I said before,' Ren began.

'Please, listen.'

'I'm not coming back,' Ren insisted.

'Hear me out.'

Ren said nothing and let Lilac continue:

'Much has been discussed. You'll be pleased to know Grist has been punished with two weeks in the 'gettory.'

Ren grimaced: 'Good. That's as it should be.'

'Saffron said he's determined to root out underhand practice. He has no liking for those that use violence.'

'Neither have I.' Ren ran her hand over a Lemon Balm, releasing the scent, watching for Lilac's response out of the corner of her eye.

Lilac gave a short laugh: 'Yes, well, he made it plain he won't tolerate the Mazards and our secret ways either.'

'So will they punish you?'

Lilac stopped walking and turned to face Ren:

'No.'

Ren couldn't believe it:

'But you broke the law - are the Gild and Council just

going to forget all about it?'

She was angry and confused. Did she want Lilac punished?

'Not if we formally renounce the Mazards.'

'I was never a real Member. They can't accuse me.'

'Ren..'

'I was forced to do your bidding!'

Lilac, her neck flushed, took a breath about to reply, then shut her mouth and walked on. Ren called after her:

'I don't act for you or the Mazards anymore.'

Lilac turned round:

'Listen Ren, there *is* interest in Azurro. Saffron agreed that ignoring a new dye wouldn't be wise. A lot of merchants share his view, and understand Samara could be a new market for our cloth. They're asking the Council to look sympathetically at Greenweed's motives for acting with the Mazards.'

'That's another thing!' Ren threw her arms in the air: 'I can't believe Greenweed was a Mazard. You both lied to me!'

'Ren, listen..'

'He said he wanted me to be your maid. What you planned was for me to be a Mazard spy, without telling me. You left me to flounder in the dark.'

Lilac smiled: 'In the dark, you searched for the light and found it.'

'What?'

'It kept you safer, from Grist's questions.'

Ren shook her head and murmured: 'Greenweed won the vote in the Gild. A small majority anyway.'

Lilac walked back to Ren and took her hands:

'Exactly! You know the Mazards had good intentions. It's

what we worked for. And the merchants are pleased by Bark's offer of trade with Samara.'

At Bark's name, Ren's heart beat faster:

'Is .. is he to be punished?'

Lilac shook her head, they walked in silence for a while.

'Captain Pallet is unhappy. He calls it *political convenience*. But Bark's father mustn't be antagonised.'

'Some say it's a Samaran plot.'

'Who?' Lilac demanded.

'Blue Hands fear it.' Ren folded her arms. 'Your father. He never supported the "Devil's Dye".'

'He was lining his own pockets, along with some Braymer merchants, keeping false accounts and sharing the profit.'

Ren shook her head, 'I can't believe that no-one is to be punished.' She would never understand the workings of power.

Lilac spoke carefully: 'My father's under supervision. As am I.'

Ren faced Lilac: 'I don't want to be your maid. Anybody's maid!'

Lilac walked ahead, Ren couldn't see her expression as she replied:

'I understand your feelings, Ren. But don't make hasty decisions.' Lilac picked a pea pod, and began to eat the peas. Ren wanted to dash them from her hands.

'Come back to the Hall, just for a while. The Council and Gild are in discussion about rewriting the Charter. Perhaps you could be part of that, the future of the Isles.'

'And - Bark?'

'He's now an official guest of the Barrow Hall.' Lilac smiled.

The thought of Bark and Lilac together up at the Hall set jealousy snaking through her. She had to go back.

As Ren set off for the Hall, she walked along the cliffs and listened to the familiar suck and roar of the surf, the seagulls crying. She took deep breaths of the salty air, light-headed, as if floating in a dream world. She saw yellow gorse covered with blue butterflies. Why wasn't this simple life enough to make her happy? As she rounded the harbour, the night she rowed Bark to the Shebble Inn came flooding back. She closed her eyes and imagined the touch of his hands, the sound of his voice, the taste of his lips. It does me no good, she told herself. Yet she was filled with a longing that nothing would dislodge, despite Moss's warnings.

Arriving at the Hall, unable to settle, she wandered in the courtyard. Bees hummed in the beds bright with May blooms: pink roses, white orange blossom. Lush greenery twisted up and over walkways to give shade, hung with clusters of tiny purple flowers. The scent was designed to create a calming atmosphere.

She sat mulling over how ignorant she'd been of the ways of the Hall, unaware of secret undercurrents. She looked up to the highest point on the roof and shuddered, thinking how Grist had threatened to throw her down. She'd done things no other Ladies' maids would: saving Bark from the 'gettory, resetting his shoulder, rowing him to meet the Alchemist. He was somewhere in the Hall, and she longed to see him, reasoning - if I'm free of my duty to Lilac, I could be by his side, help him. Why shouldn't I? I'm ready for anything now.

She sensed another presence watching her. Her heart leapt as she saw a figure through the leaves. Had she conjured Bark with her longing? The figure moved into sunlight - Lady Rose approached her frowning. Rose stood a moment then said:

'You're looking better than I expected.'

Ren half-smiled. Rose sat on a bench and patted the seat beside her.

'You did - well. In your evidence giving.'

Ren turned to her in surprise.

'You kept our - my - part in it from the public.' Rose inclined her head: 'Thank you.' She spoke in an undertone. 'The whole Barrow Hall has been upset about this sad sorry matter.'

Rose sighed and sat back.

'Are you back at the Hall for good?'

Ren shrugged.

'Take what opportunities are offered. The world is changing. You're proof of that.'

Was that a compliment, Ren wondered. Rose seemed to grow smaller, her eyes distant:

'Lilac was right. My skills and purpose are becoming out of step.'

'No, no - you taught me well.' As she said it, Ren knew it was true.

Rose stiffened, the intimate mood gone.

'The delegates are to depart for Samara tomorrow. There will be a formal banquet tonight. You are requested to attend.'

Ren's eyes lit up: 'My first banquet.'

'Quite so. Please wear your best dress. Try to behave with decorum. The occasion demands it.' Rose left and didn't see Ren do a little twirl. This would be her opportunity to see Bark, her chance to dazzle him.

Smiling, she returned to her room to prepare for the evening. First, Ren shook out her best silk dress, for state occasions and never worn. She held the fabric to her cheek, loving its cool lustre: greeny blue Popinjay was her favourite colour. She let it hang to lose any creases. She bathed herself, and washed her hair in rosemary water. She took care over her nails, cleaning and trimming them. While her long brown hair dried, she wandered in the courtyard, collecting blossoms. That evening she swept her hair up, and wove a coronet with the flowers, singing to herself. Finally she laced up the dress as tight as it would go, giving plumpness to her breasts, bit her lips and pinched her cheeks to make them red. She was ready. Excitement coursed through her.

The walls were hung with ivy and greenery. Candles stood around the edges of the Hall, tapers lit up every table covered in pale blue linen, with posies set among the forks and napkins. The whole space shimmered with light. Heads turned as she entered the Hall. She blushed, walking with her head high and her back straight but her eyes were darting around, longing to catch a glimpse of Bark, for him to see her in the beautiful clothes.

All the merchants and courtiers, members of the Hall and even the actors were there, returned from their tour of the Isles. Her heart leapt as she saw him next to Count Saffron, on the top table with Charlatan, Master Greenweed and Lilac glowing in the light of their crystal goblets. He looked more handsome than ever, in a long robe of blue silk, his dark hair curling down his neck, a silver and blue pendant hanging on his chest.

With a light step, she approached the top table. She was stopped by a nip of sharp nails to her hand and Lady Rose hissed in her ear:

'You sit with the other Ladies' maids.'

Ren turned away, humiliated. She wanted to disappear. Far from the top table, she sat with her head down, tears pricking her eyes. What a fool, to think she could - Moss was right.

When the Hall was full and everyone seated, the Governor, stoney-faced, stood on the dais and called for attention. Count Saffron and Bark came to join him.

'I hereby present you, Count Saffron of Calico, our Delegate to Samara, with letters of introduction from the Council of Five. I present you, Bark, with these bolts of fine kersey cloth, a jeroboam of Calico wine and a carving of the Shebble shell, the ancient symbol of our Isle, as gifts for the Overlord of Samara. You are both charged with making entreaties, on our behalf, to the Overlord of Samara for the acquisition of the plant known as Azurro.'

He asked the assembled courtiers to drink a toast of good health. Everyone raised a glass, and drank a mouthful of cool Calico wine.

Formalities over, the banquet began.

Chapter 15
The Banquet

Sitting with the maids Ren realised how little she knew any of them: Lilac had isolated her, keeping her close to her side. She wasn't surprised the women round the table didn't include her in conversation as they chattered about other courtiers, the food, and their clothes. They mistrusted her, especially since the hearing, and she had little in common to talk about. Like Lilac, she'd flouted the rules of social behaviour. If they did glance at her, they turned away when she met their eyes and they'd whisper, heads together. So when Dainty, the boy actor, slipped in beside her, her heart lifted.

He touched her dress:

'That's a beauty, and so are you, Ren.'

She smiled: 'Thank you - it would suit you too.'

They both laughed.

Dainty was popular with the maids, teasing and flirting easily and keeping them all in fits of laughter with riddles and quotations from plays. His arrival melted the frosty mood toward Ren. Some even spoke to her, but her mind was elsewhere. Ren's eyes strayed often to the top table, watching Bark, and her ears strained for any talk. She smiled at Dainty, but inside her heart was hurting. She couldn't rouse much appetite although the food kept coming, in such number and variety of dishes it sickened her: whole fish served on beds of samphire, stewed coney, wilted greens with chook eggs.

There were flagons of Calico mead and cold pewter flasks of white wine on every table, and Ren drank without thinking; it numbed the hurt. The banquet ended with pickled plums, Herd Island cheese and doughy rolls. Astonished that people could eat so much, even though the portions were small, she remarked to Dainty:

'This is more than enough to live on for a week.'

'Eat it and be thankful. You may go hungry tomorrow.' He winked and pocketed a couple of rolls.

'I'll never feel hungry again.'

Anger and misery chased round her: she wished she was back at home, not dressed up in silks with flowers in her hair. She hated banquets! Then she heard Charlatan's laughter over the chatter of the Hall and stared, longing to be sitting with them, listening to their conversation. As the candles burned low, Charlatan stood and called:

'Ladies and Gentles - we would like to add some entertainment to the evening.'

To applause and shouts of approval, Charlatan waved his arm and Dainty stood up, whispering to her:

'Now I must pay for my supper.'

He went and mounted the dais. Even wearing breeches, his curly hair and smooth skin gave him the look of a girl. He bowed to the gathered guests and announced:

'This is an old Braymer song. You have a similar on Calico, called Hard Fortune.'

He lifted his face and began in a pure, haunting voice.

Young girls, take warning, take warning from me,
Never place your affections on a young man so free,

They will hug you and kiss you and tell you more lies,
Than the waves on the sea or the stars in the sky.

His voice wound its way into her thoughts, matching her mood, holding her in its melody.

Oh, meeting's a pleasure and parting's a grief,
And a false-hearted lover is worse than a thief,
For a thief will just rob you and take what you have,
But a false-hearted lover will make you his slave.

He'll call you his darling, he'll call you his pearl,
And go behind you with some other girl;
He'll promise to love you and make you his wife,
Then leave you down-hearted for the rest of your life.

She looked up at Bark. He was gazing at her. He gave her the most dazzling smile: her stomach somersaulted, and in her head she dismissed Moss's warning voice.

Finally the banquet and festivities were over. The feasters were drifting away, the kitchen staff tidying up. Ren stood, a little giddy, hanging back as she saw the group from the top table move off together. Then Bark turned and beckoned to her. Heart fluttering, she patted Dainty's arm and kissed his cheek: 'Goodnight. Thank you for the sad song.'

'I sang it for you, Ren. Take care of yourself.' He went off back to The Starfish moored on the quay. Ren turned, lifting her skirts, and hurried to catch up with Charlatan and Greenweed, as Lilac and Bark were climbing the stairs. She thought at first they were going to Lilac's room, but they went on up, and she guessed they were climbing to the Lookout tower. She whispered to Charlatan:

'What's going on?'

'A last meeting of the Mazards, dear girl.' He tapped his nose.

'Surely there's no need for secrecy anymore?'

'That's correct.' Greenweed smiled at her. 'I believe we're about to disband the society.'

'A little bit of ceremony adds a sense of occasion, don't you think?' Charlatan waved his arm. 'And I must say you look just the part.' He twirled his moustache and Greenweed nodded in agreement. She smiled, light-headed, her pulse racing.

They came out onto the small turret, crowded together under the starry canopy. Ren squeezed in beside Bark. No-one spoke. The moon's silvery path led away to the horizon. The night noises of the town drifted up: a man's laughter, donkey bells tinkling, a woman calling, far away, like another world below. The air smelled of sun-warmed stone and coconut gorse. Ren secretly fingered the silk of Bark's robe, picturing his body so close it sent shivers down her spine. She had to bite her tongue to stop herself speaking his name.

Finally Lilac sighed:

'This is the end. The purpose of our group has been greatly advanced. And we've made promises to the Council of Five. We must renounce our membership of the Mazards.'

The men nodded. Ren just watched.

'We now disband the Mazards. From henceforth we will not meet or act in secret, against the wishes of the Council of Calico. Agreed?'

Everyone murmured: 'Agreed.'

'However,' she continued in a more conspiratorial tone, 'we must still honour our vow of silence on past activities. If no-one asks, we do no wrong by saying nothing, I think. Charlatan, Bark, Greenweed?' Lilac turned to her, 'Ren?'

Lilac held out her hands. Ren, between Charlatan and Bark, grasped both of theirs. She wanted to laugh for joy as Bark's hand squeezed hers in the darkness. They swore the oath, smiled at each other and made their way down into the corridors of the Hall.

Lilac curtsied 'Goodnight' and disappeared off in one direction. Bark hesitated, talking with Charlatan and Greenweed but with Ren's hand still held firmly in his. She thought her heart would burst. Finally Charlatan and Greenweed bade them goodnight.

'Come,' Bark pulled her.

Breathing quick and shallow she followed him to his room. He shut the door, and in the dark held her, kissing her lips, her eyes, her forehead, muttering: 'You're magnificent.'

She swept his hair back: 'Is your forehead mended?'

He looked at her, nodding. 'Is all well?'

She put her arms round his waist, drawing him close:

'Now I'm with you.'

He stroked her hair: 'I brought you here -' He was going to speak more, she put a finger to his lips, leaned in and kissed him.

He returned her kiss then he drew back:

'I'm leaving tomorrow. I wanted to say goodbye.'

Her face lit up: 'I'll come with you!'

Bark searched her face and said nothing.

'I no longer serve Lilac. I could be yours.'

Slowly, he shook his head.

'I want to be with you,' she insisted.

He turned away: 'I'm sorry Ren. There's no place for you in my company.'

He moved to the window and stood looking out at the sky, rich with stars. She joined him, staring at the night:

'I saved you many times over, remember? You need me!' She laughed and turned to him. He caught her into an embrace. Ren, reckless and joyful, saw herself by his side as they left Barrow Hall far behind. They clung to each other a while, then Bark sighed, drew back and stroked her cheek.

He reached out and gently took the flowers one by one from her hair, letting them fall about her shoulders. He unpinned her hair, lifted a strand and it drifted through his fingers. She took his hands and kissed the palms and the inside of his wrists, breathing in the smell of his skin.

He drew her close. She closed her eyes as he kissed her, caressing her neck.

He stopped and sighed:

'This isn't why I brought you here. We mustn't.'

Opening her eyes she searched his face. He was what she wanted. He would be hers, she would make him want her. She kissed him. He didn't move. She kissed his cheeks and brushed her lips over his eyelashes. She kissed his neck and let her tongue lick and suck his ear lobes, arousing his desire, arousing her own. He groaned, and pulled at the laces of her bodice. She touched his hands as they worked. He opened her chemise, revealing her breasts. A pink flush rose up her chest and neck. She slipped her chemise over her head and brought his fingers to her breasts. She sighed as he kissed them and took her nipple in his mouth. Fumbling with her skirt, she let it slip down until she was naked. He stood and gazed at her; she felt her body blaze like a ray of light.

Then he put a hand to his forehead:

'No. This is wrong.'

She took his hand and led him to his bed. She kissed his mouth, pushing against him.

She hauled up his robes and lifted them off, letting them drop to the ground. His pendant swung into her face and caught in her hair, they laughed as she untangled it. His brown body glistened in the starlight. She was bold with desire, kissing his chest, his shoulders and arms. Her fingers were greedy for his skin. He watched her lay her palms on his chest and draw them down to his hips, exploring these new parts of him, the soft hair, the hardness. She pulled him to the bed and he lay down beside her. She wanted this wild danger more than anything she'd ever wanted.

Taking his hand, she drew it down to her thighs. He explored her with his fingers, and she gasped with pleasure. They kissed again and again, their mouths open. She whispered his name like a spell, holding him close, her skin slick and slippery against his. Then he was lying on top of her, heavy, and smelling of wine. Her breath squashed out of her by his weight, she pulled away, gasping for air. She realised he was the worse for drink. His leg forced between her thighs, opening her up, pinning her down. She kept embracing him, stroking his back, wanting him to be slow and careful but he was eager, pushing roughly into her tender flesh.

He pushed again and she bit her lip; he was too heavy, she couldn't change her position. He moved harder, faster. Even though she felt it like a razor clam scouring her, she didn't stop him. He wanted her. He was under her spell - this was her power. She watched him, his head back, his eyes closed, breathing hard, miles away. Abruptly he moaned and lay still, his face buried in her shoulder.

She had her wish.

He rolled onto his back and was soon snoring. Lying awake, she was aware of his body, hot in slumber beside her, so desirable, so alien. Yet doubt edged her triumph: had he already tried and tired of Lilac? Was he loving both of them?

No, Bark had chosen her, not Lilac. She knew his desire for her was strong, and she'd made it happen, overcoming his reluctance. Should she have been more careful, stopped him before his final moment? Had she done it on purpose? A confused thrill went through her - he was about to sail a thousand leagues away to another world. If she conceived Bark's child, it would be a link that could never be broken. She didn't care what anyone said, she'd find a way to go with him.

As dawn light crept through the curtains, Ren woke to find herself alone. She stretched, calling Bark's name. No reply came. His silver and blue pendant was lying on a chair, underneath it was a note. She jumped up, and read:

'To remember me by.' She gripped the jewel to her breast, breathing fast.

She threw on her clothes and ran down to the harbour. Bark, dressed in his seaman's outfit, was loading provisions for the journey. He dusted his hands and came down the gangplank.

She ran to him:

'I thought you'd gone,' she cried 'and I'd never see you.' She put her hands out towards him. He stepped back, holding her at arms length.

'You shouldn't have come.'

She collapsed, tears flowing:

'I thought we'd be together.'

Pulling her up, he said:

'It's not possible. It was never possible.'

She held on to his hands, her voice choking.

He relented, taking her in his arms. He wiped tears from her eyes and spoke quietly into her ear.

'I'm sorry. I did wrong - last night..'

'But you wanted me. We're meant to be together, why not?'

'Be brave.' He kissed her, and let her go. She threw her arms round his neck, holding tight, searching his face:

'Please. Let me come with you.'

Shrugging off her grasp, he hefted a box onto his shoulder. Blind with tears, she whispered:

'Don't leave me.'

He walked up the gangway onto the ship without another word.

An hour later she stood, red-eyed from weeping, with Lilac and a crowd on the quayside, for the ceremony of the Sailing of the Trade Delegation.

Lilac adjusted her skirts, the plain underskirt and then the heavy brocade for special Sailings, and a cloak of indigo with silver stars surrounding one hand with a shell inset. On the harbour, she pronounced the words:

'Friends; Let the wind blow from East to Home and the water be sweet on this voyage. We wish her well.'

The gangplank was withdrawn. Bark, busy with ropes and sails, never looked back at the quay.

'Come along,' Lilac urged Ren, but she didn't hear. She stood, holding Bark's pendant tight in her pocket, until the ship was a dot on the horizon.

That evening, Lilac called Ren to her room:

'I don't know why I didn't see it before. You've fallen under Bark's spell.'

She reached out and took Ren's hand.

'He charms everyone, there's no shame or foolishness in your feelings. But you must understand - he's a king's son. He would never have dealings with a woman of low rank.'

Ren withdrew her hand from Lilac's:

'If he's a king's son, he can do as he chooses.'

Lilac shook her head:

'His life is mapped out by forces other than his own will. Great nobility's accompanied by onerous duties. It's been arranged since he was a boy - he's betrothed.'

Ren paled.

'His wife-to-be is still a young girl, the daughter of a powerful Lord.'

'Betrothed isn't the same as married. He could choose again.'

'It's his father's choice. He must obey.'

A black mist came over Ren. She flew out of the room, running away from Lilac, away from the Hall, away from everything.

She ran down alleys and streets blindly, one thought worming through her mind: he used me, he used me and never loved me. She found herself at the harbour, surrounded by seaweed smells, roasting fish and garlic. There were couples walking, folk laughing, men drinking, beckoning her - too many people, too much life. She ran down to the cold, empty strand and sobbed into the night air. She shivered, all alone in the meaningless cosmos.

Why had he made love to her? What if he did love her? It was no use. He had to marry someone else, someone he didn't love. He could never be with Ren, ever. Moss was right. Her chest ached, truly her heart was broken. Her life was over. The stars watched her, distant and mocking, the sea was cold and indifferent. She walked to the edge of the ocean, indigo, endless. Somewhere out there was Bark's ship, taking him away for ever. She needed to stop this pain, this emptiness, to punish her foolish heart.

She waded in, letting the waves suck and pull at her dress. As the material soaked up water it grew heavier, her steps slower. She held out her arms and stood, shaking, crying into the night. A wave toppled her into the cold. She gulped and spluttered, swallowing salty mouthfuls. Coughing, she struggled to stand with her wet clothes, trying to turn to the shore. Another wave knocked her and she went under. The current pulled her, water swept up her nose and down her throat. She fought against the current, but couldn't resist the suck downwards. Sinking, sinking down in to the dark cold ocean. She couldn't hear, couldn't see, couldn't think. Her mind closed down, oblivion beckoned.

But her body rebelled: with lungs bursting, her chest clamoured for air. Panic-stricken, her legs kicked as her feet tangled in swirling cloth. Reaching out, she clawed for the surface, getting no purchase on the sea. Her efforts dissolved, her limbs lost the battle, her last thought - I'm drowned.

The next she knew, she'd been lifted on a powerful wave and thrown down hard onto sand. It left her there, winded. Alive. She vomited sea water. Another wave battered down on her, threatening to drag her back to the black depths. She dug her fingers into the sand, crawled a little way up the beach, her chest heaving, then collapsed, feeling the cold grit on her cheek, her wet clothing weighing her down. She didn't move.

There was a far-off cry. Someone was calling her name. It was shouted again. She didn't care, had no energy to speak. Her eyes stayed closed.

'Is she breathing?'

'She's half-drowned!'

'Ren! Ren, can you hear me?'

Her eyes flickered.

'She's alive.' Hands pulled her up into a sitting position.

214

She coughed violently, and vomited more water.

'Leave me.' She slumped forward.

'Don't be daft.'

'You can't stay here, Ren.'

They bent her over, and slapped her back, forcing her to cough up water again. The darkness surrounded her, pulling her down to sleep. She slipped sideways.

'Come on. You'll die of cold. Take her arm, Nutmeg.'

'I've got her m'Lady. Heave!'

They pulled her up, until she was standing. Lilac wiped the hair from Ren's face.

'I thought I'd lost you.'

Chapter 16
Sailing

'No - don't. I, I failed - everything..'

Ren stuttered through chattering teeth, trying to escape their hold.

Lilac and Nutmeg had her between them, stumbling back along the beach, Nutmeg urging her along:

'You need a good hot cup o' summat.'

They got her back to the harbour and into the Shebble Inn. Mrs Dogfish banked up the fire and brought a blanket.

'Oh dear me, your family are in the wars. First Vetch and now you.'

Ren stood, letting Mrs Dogfish take off her soaking cloak, unlace her dress, and wrap her with the woollen blanket. It smelled of sweet woodsmoke, of home. Tears trickled down her cheeks.

'Did you have an accident?' Mrs Dogfish asked.

In shock, Ren was too dazed to speak sense. A violent shivering fit took hold of her. They sat her by the fire and gave her a brandy laced with honey and talked in hushed tones. As she sipped, her clothes steamed over the back of a chair, and words and phrases floated into her consciousness - 'upset' 'a difficult time' 'she's tired' 'a Blue Hand, up at the Hall..'

Then she heard her name: 'Ren?' then more loudly: 'Ren!' She stared at Lilac.

'Shall I send Dogfish to fetch your mother?' Lilac asked.

She couldn't speak, her teeth were chattering so badly, and just shook her head.

Nutmeg knelt by her, warming her cold hands in her own. Lilac put an arm around her, rubbing her.

'I'm sorry. I should have..' Lilac's voice broke a little. 'This is my fault.'

Ren stared at her feet, embarrassed by all their kind attention, stiff and awkward in Lilac's arms, trying hard not to cry, but tears dripped off her nose and cheeks.

'There, there dear.' Mrs Dogfish spoke soothingly. 'You're safe now.'

Ren said nothing, but relented a little, and leant into Lilac's warm body, letting herself be comforted. As she warmed up, her cheeks grew pink, and her eyelids began to droop.

Once again, Ren found herself in the little bedroom upstairs at the Shebble Inn. By the light of a single candle flame Lilac sat watching over her. She laid a tentative hand on Ren and bent closer:

'Is there something you want to tell me?'

Ren shook her head as tears leaked out of the corners of her eyes, dampening the pillow.

She turned on her side away from Lilac. Her kindness and concern were too much, and too late. Lilac wasn't her friend, and she wasn't Lilac's social equal. There was a gulf that kept them apart. She wasn't going to tell her about Bark. That was her own precious secret and keeping quiet was her one power.

She closed her eyes, ignoring Lilac's words of explanation:

'Bark is handsome, persuasive. I'm not surprised you were flattered by his attentions. But he was wrong if he gave you any sign of encouragement. He comes from a very different culture, their attitudes to women are...'

Ren drifted off.

The next morning she woke shamefaced, wanting to get away, finding Lilac's concern more difficult to accept than her criticism.

'I'm sorry I put you to this bother. I'll go home now.'

'Please. Come back to the Hall.' Lilac gave her an awkward smile. 'I'd like you to. And I'm afraid you're still required to.'

She dressed in her salt-stained clothes, creased but dry, and thought what a sorry state she must look. She wouldn't eat anything, but drank a hot tea. Lilac thanked Mrs Dogfish and paid her for her services, although she insisted she didn't want money, and was glad to help. Before they stepped out, Ren turned to Mrs Dogfish:

'Please. Promise me you won't say anything about this to Vetch or Moss, or, or any Blue Hands. I don't want my mother to hear of it.'

Mrs Dogfish nodded, serious:

'You have my word, my dear. Now, you promise me you'll take care of yourself?'

Lilac and Ren parted with Mrs Dogfish at the inn door. Ren didn't look back. Her steps slow, her spirit crushed.

At the Hall, with no other options, Ren went back to her

duties, just as Moss had predicted. She performed them in a listless manner - some mornings she could hardly drag herself out of bed and she only picked at food as her appetite waned. Her heart was not in her work and her mind was elsewhere. She brought Lilac meals, she kept her room tidy, and mended and sewed as before, but she only half-listened to instructions or conversations and forgot what they were about.

Lilac was often busy at meetings; then Ren would drift to the Library and sit staring at a map of Samara, or lie on her bed, daydreaming, Bark's pendant in her pocket.

* * *

One morning, Lilac was talking and Ren's attention was caught by the mention of Bark's name.

'He'll be gone for the summer and will return by November, when we hope he'll have answers about trading Azurro with us.'

Silence hung in the air as both women considered this. Ren stared - it hadn't occurred to her that perhaps Lilac was suffering too, that she might feel the same. Had Bark courted Lilac, promised her more than he could give? Was Lilac aching inside, longing for him, his voice, his touch, to have him by her side?

'Why didn't you go to Samara?'

There was a pause, Lilac cleared her throat:

'The Samaran's won't trade with women. They keep their own locked away.'

Silence stretched between them again. Against her will, she found a little space opening in her heart to feel sorry for

Lilac, her jealousy tempered by this realisation.

Lilac sighed:

'Ren. Are you paying attention?'

'What? I'm sorry my Lady.'

'I'd like you to be my Notary.'

Ren's thoughts were still far away. She couldn't make sense of the words.

'To assist me, take notes, keep my books in order.'

Ren's mouth opened and closed, nothing came out.

'You've learnt much and experienced more in the last few months. Your speech to the Blue Hands - people are still talking about it.' Lilac stood up and fiddled with a pile of papers. 'Many older, more scholarly men wouldn't speak without a prepared speech. You spoke from the heart.'

Ren sat, staring into the distance as Lilac struggled to express herself:

'I - I, have much to learn from you. You understand the Blue Hands. It's why I picked you in the first place.' Lilac looked away: 'When I thought I'd nearly lost you - .' She turned back: 'I'd be a fool to let you go. You see Ren, it's been proposed I take part in the development of Azurro.'

'You?'

Lilac nodded: 'The Council accept that I already have some knowledge and experience. So they've offered me a special role. The first woman so highly placed. I thought, why not have another woman to aid me? We work well together, don't we?'

Lilac recovered her old fire and enthusiasm:

'Imagine. This could be the beginning of a new era

of trade and exchange for the Gild and the Isles - a great challenge.'

'What special role?'

'To talk to the Wool and Silk merchants about Azurro, persuade them Samara could be a rich trading opportunity. In preparation for rewriting the Gild Articles and the Trade Charter.'

Ren said nothing, watching Lilac.

'Of course, I don't want to force you. It must be your choice, truly.' Lilac flushed. 'But you could be so much more than just a maid.'

Ren hesitated a long while. She had to admit she couldn't go back to being a Blue Hand, thinking of Tern, certain many workers were angry at what they saw as her betrayal. She wouldn't be welcome. If she wasn't a Blue Hand anymore and she'd failed as a maid, who was she?

Lilac broke through her thoughts:

'Ren? I'd like you to assume the responsibilities straight away. If you're agreeable, that is.'

Still Ren hesitated.

'Greenweed has asked that we help discuss the drawing up of the new Charter, too, when I have convinced the Braymer merchants, obviously.'

This jolted Ren out of her silence:

'You mean to go to Braymer, my Lady?'

'I'll sail with Charlatan and the actors. It'll take a month at sea.' Lilac paused:

'I'd like you to come with me.'

* * *

The sun warmed the front of the cottage with a buttery light, as if the world was full of joy. How could the sun keep shining, the tide rise and fall when Ren's world had come to a stop? She hesitated to enter.

Fern's voice rang out: 'Look who's here!' as she came round the side of the house with a bucket of water. Fern opened the door and Ren followed. She sat while her mother roused the fire and set water to boil. Vetch came in with firewood.

'Well?' her mother said, halfway between a question and an exclamation. 'Peppermint tea?'

Ren nodded. Vetch stacked the wood and asked over his shoulder:

'How's Lady Lilac? Happy it's all over, I expect.'

She looked away out of the small window: 'All over,' echoing his words.

'What about you?' Fern asked.

Ren sat there looking from one to the other.

'Lilac has asked that I be her Notary.'

Fern's eyebrows rose in twin arches:

'Notary is it?' she breathed. 'Well well. That's..'

'A great responsibility.' Vetch spoke in admiration.

'Oh, I don't know. I'm not sure.'

Fern gave a shrewd look: 'Lilac wouldn't have asked if she didn't think you were capable.'

Ren looked at her mother's worn face, smiling at her.

'I suppose so.'

'Suppose nothing. Mother's right,' Vetch said.

'She wants me to go to Braymer.'

223

Fern exchanged glances with Vetch, and said:

'This is a new opportunity.'

'It's so far away, from you.'

Vetch, smiling, nudged her and she laughed for the first time since her rescue from the waves.

She knew they were right. She'd accept Lilac's offer - why stay at home? The one person her heart ached for had left Calico. At the back of her mind was a tiny thought - a chance of contact with Bark, sometime in the future.

Although she tried not to think of him, ever since that night with Bark, Ren was alert to every twinge and change in her body. With a mixture of dread and excitement she counted and recounted the days, anticipating her Flowers. Were her breasts tender, did her skirt feel tight, was her stomach refusing food? Then she'd tell herself she was being ridiculous, it was too soon to tell. Anyway, it was just the once, it was unlikely she'd fallen. She didn't feel any different. And if she did - well, it was because her mood was low. Now she had an unexpected new future opening up, she felt more alive, and told herself to put misery behind her.

It was the end of May when The Starfish was due to sail, after the final celebration of the month - the Blue Hands' Festival. Each year, a different lad from the Sheds was chosen to prepare the Dancing Field, and then had the honour of leading the Dye girls in procession. This year, to Ren's delight, it was Vetch.

Kale scythed the field; Ren helped Vetch set out square

boards in the space. They put tin holders down, each with a candle - five hundred kept for the purpose. Once the space was prepared, they went home to eat a last family meal all together - garlic fish stew and fresh greens from the allotment, and a special custard made from chook eggs: Ren's favourite dish. Then, dressed in his best shirt and breeches, his stunted arm in a sling of bright bandanna scarves, Vetch, his mother and Ren returned to the Dancing Fields as the sun was sliding down to set. Folk were gathering, picking their places to sit on the grass, to get a good view of the spectacle. Kale sat down beside Ren and her mother.

'I'm glad to see Vetch well again and in good spirits.'

He looked at Ren:

'And you. Going up in the world. I always knew you were special.'

She blushed and looked away. Kale was so kind, he didn't deserve his fate. Who did?

At eight o'clock, Vetch, holding hands with Moss, led the Dye girls in procession into the Dancing Fields. They wore full skirts, looped and tied to their waists, clogs, cambric shirts and bandannas round their necks. Each girl held a lit taper: they arrived as a wavering line of flames coming through the dusk. Folk clapped and called out until all the girls were in the dancing square. Vetch called:

'Let the Blue Hands begin!'

The girls knelt and lit two candles, then formed themselves into a large circle and began to sing. The crowd was silent as the young women's voices harmonised into the evening air. Next, a fiddle player struck up a fast jig, accompanied by a wide drum beaten with a two-headed spindle that kept a pounding beat. The girls performed a hand-holding dance, weaving in and out. Excitement mounted as girls began to clog dance on the boards, and the watchers clapped along. So they carried on dancing into the night, a swirling flash of figures lit by candle light. Well past midnight was a final song, a Calico lullaby sung in close three-part harmony, marking the end of May and the Blue Hand Festival. Ren watched with a mixture of pleasure and regret.

'Do you miss all this?' Kale nodded towards the dancing girls.

'I don't feel part of that world. I wonder if I ever really did.'

'Like me. I don't know where I belong.' He looked sad. 'When you can't work, what use are you?'

She put an arm round him: 'Maybe things will be better, there'll be other chances.'

Kale shrugged: 'Come on, I'll walk you home'.

The next day, with the tide right, Ren and Lilac were down at the harbour preparing for the sailing. Charlatan welcomed them on board and Dainty showed Ren to a cabin. He demonstrated how to use a hammock, which made her laugh and say she'd prefer to sleep on the flat planks. She had one small trunk containing her belongings: Bark's pendant, the tools of the Notary's trade - quill, ink and paper, and her clothes, including her newly-tailored Notary outfit. Unlike her softer pink maid's dresses, this was a sage green brocade bodice and skirt, stiff and formal.

Lilac was more familiar with sailing, and wasted no time having her luggage and boxes of papers stowed in her own, larger cabin.

There was a small group at the harbour to see them off. Ren dressed in her green outfit and Lilac wore her indigo cloak with stars for the occasion. With Saffron gone to Samara, Lilac's father, the Governor and Greenweed stood as formal representatives of Calico. The Governor gave Lilac a letter:

'For Master Tawney. Please see that he receives it personally.'

Lilac nodded, and the Governor embraced her but didn't smile.

Greenweed gave Ren the carefully wrapped Azurro cloth.

'This will be an important part of your evidence to the merchants in Braymer. Lilac insisted that you take responsibility for it.' He embraced her, and spoke so only she could hear: 'Take care, my dear. Your father would be proud. I have every confidence in you.'

Then he shook Lilac's hand and Charlatan's.

Ren hugged her mother and Vetch. Kale kissed her:

'You look important!' He smiled.

'Take care.' Moss hugged her for a long time.

Lilac and Ren boarded, and stood together with Charlatan at the rail as the gangplank was pulled up and the ship weighed anchor.

Ren noticed Tern standing with Grist on the quay. She pointed:

227

'Grist is out of the 'gettory.'

'Not happy news.' Charlatan twisted his moustache.

Lilac agreed. Ren nodded, and as the ship edged away from the quayside, she watched Tern deep in conversation, wondering what business he might have with Grist.

The sun was high, the water sparkling and lively. Ren found the shifting motion of the ship was beginning to make her nauseous.

'Ah, 'tis the sea malady!' Charlatan clapped her on the back.

'You'll get used to it.' Lilac reassured her.

'We'll keep you entertained. Strike up a tune!' Charlatan cried. 'Makepiece?'

One of the actors began a soulful tune on the hurdy-gurdy.

It filled her ears as she leant on the rail, watching her town, the familiar coastline, shrink and become indistinct. Ren had never been this far from home before, cut adrift from family and everyday life. She had leagues to go before she'd reach land again. It was a strange new journey.

If you've enjoyed *Ren and the Blue Hands,* please read *Chapter 1 - Braymer,* of the next book in the trilogy, '*Ren and the Blue Cloth'* on the following page.

Ren and the Blue Cloth

Chapter 1
Braymer

The ship lurched, Ren put a hand out to steady herself. Her insides were crawling up her throat.

'Here,'

Dainty offered a cup of water from a barrel on deck: 'It's important to replace fluid when you lose it.'

'Yes nurse.' She rested her forehead on the edge of the rail.

Dainty handed her a kerchief to wipe her mouth. She turned away quickly and heaved as another bout of nausea gripped:

'Oh,' she groaned, 'I'll die.'

'No-one dies of sea sickness - they just wish they could.' He laid a hand on her back. 'You should try and eat.' He went below and reappeared with a hunk of bread, and broke off a piece: 'Here, just a mouthful.'

After a week at sea, she'd begun to believe there was no end to the ocean, or her nausea. Feeling sick was like keeping a secret: she felt wretched, couldn't think of anything but wanting to get rid of it, yet fearful of that moment too. Ren thought she was done with keeping secrets when she set sail from Calico, now she knew how wrong she'd been.

She stayed on deck in the fresh air as much as possible, where the actors kept her mind off her worries, as the endless days merged into one another.

She was sitting on a thick pile of rope, Needle crosslegged beside her with a costume on his lap, making repairs, and Dainty lying full stretch on the deck, eyes closed. Makepiece arrived with his hurdy-gurdy, and Dainty called:

'Makepiece! Make us merry.'

'I cannot promise to, my fingers follow their own way, and merry tunes can sometimes make us sad, I fear.'

Needle complained:

'If he plays a reel, my needle wants to dance a jig faster than my eyes. I prefer a slow tune.'

Makepiece turned the handle, the drone picked up, and he began to play.

'How long before we stand on solid ground again?' Ren asked, of no-one in particular. Dainty laughed and said:

'Another three weeks. Patience.'

Three weeks to make a decision.

* * *

For the midday meal, the ship's company sat at long tables with benches either side. Ren sat with Lady Lilac, next to her was Charlatan, Actor Manager of the theatre troupe, then Dainty the boy actor and the rest of the theatre company, opposite the crew. It was dim in the mess deck: tallow lanterns slung above the tables threw down an oily light. Cook produced a rich fish stew. The smell made Ren's stomach turn over. As she tried to bring the spoon to her lips, there was a terrible roiling in her belly. She clamped her teeth and sat quiet.

Charlatan ate heartily: 'I insist you come to the Playing

House as my guests and see us perform in our proper home.'

Lady Lilac smiled: 'We should like that.'

Dainty leaned across to Ren: 'And I could show you some of the sights of Braymer. Would you like to visit a Threading Shed?'

Lilac interrupted: 'We'll be busy with official matters, Ren.'

Ren said nothing. She needed to lie down again.

She heard Lilac saying as she left:

'She'll manage. Everyone gets it on their first voyage.'

It was a blustery day and Ren was leaning on the deck rail staring at the endless white spume arrowing from the bow. Her hair escaped from her coif, and blew across her face. As she listened to the rushing of the water, one hand clutched her cloak shut, the other clutched the side of the ship as it rose and dipped.

An arm hooked through hers. It was Charlatan:

'Come along, you've been tied to that rail for too long.'

He forced her to walk round the deck.

'Sea biscuit?' He produced a small hard square. She took it, sucking on it to soften the dryness.

'It doesn't taste of much,' she mumbled.

'Ah, sailors swear by its life-saving properties! I've grown fond of it on my travels.'

'Have you seen many countries?'

'With the Chancellor's Men? We are world-renowned - we don't just come to your little Isles of Calico.' He laughed and waved his arm in different directions: 'The Borderlands, Frank Land, the cold Ice Country.'

'Have you been to Samara?' she asked, looking up at him. He paused.

'With the Actors? No...no.'

'Why are you called the Chancellor's men?'

'He's our Patron, our Seal of Approval. His coat of arms opens doors, respected at the highest levels.'

Ren bit on the softened biscuit: 'Our Governor didn't like you.'

Charlatan burst out laughing: 'Not a great lover of the arts.'

'He didn't like the Mazards either.'

He stopped laughing: 'Yes, well. We're done with them, eh?' He smiled again. 'I can tell you're a discerning theatre lover. Tell me, what are your favourite plays?' And he kept her walking and talking, taking her mind off the constant shifting, inside and out.

That night, down on the lower deck, on her little pallet, she pulled the blanket over her head to shut out the lanterns swaying or anything that showed the movement of the ship, taking small shallow breaths that didn't unsettle her stomach. She imagined Bark, somewhere on this same ocean, going in the opposite direction a thousand miles away. She pictured him as he was on their last night, clothed in indigo silk. From under the pillow she took the blue and silver pendant that he'd left for her, remembering it against his brown-skinned chest and how it had caught in her hair. She brought it to her nose, hoping for his scent.

As she lay there in the dim light of the under deck, she

heard a voice:

'Ren?'

It was Dainty. He sat down and put a hand out. 'How are you?'

She held his hand, but didn't answer.

'It isn't sea malady, is it?'

She lay there, her eyes closed: 'Do the others know?'

'The actors are discreet. They'd never say.'

She looked up into Dainty's kind face. If he'd guessed, had Lilac? No, Lilac was absorbed in her own plans, and anyway she would never imagine it possible that Bark would be intimate with someone like Ren, she'd said as much.

Dainty spoke softly: 'I can help.'

Ren stared at him: 'How?'

'I know a woman. Farah. Lots of girls go to her.'

'What will she do?'

'She'll help you. She works in a tavern the actors use.'

'Is it dangerous?'

'In the tavern? No.'

'No. I mean, what this woman does - to the girls.'

Dainty sighed: 'Many women have done it.' He paused: 'What would you do otherwise?'

Ren stared up into the wooden beams of the ship: 'I don't know.'

At home it would have been simple - she'd marry Kale, she'd have the child and no-one would question anything. But she was leagues from home, on her own and only Dainty knew her secret.

* * *

'Land Ho!'

The day was cold, the sky overcast, not like the heart-warming blue of Calico. Ren wrapped herself in a cloak, although it was midsummer. They'd been travelling steadily north, and Lilac had warned that Braymer had a more 'uncertain' climate than their island. The sailor up the mast had a spyglass and was pointing. She strained her eyes but couldn't make out the land. She went back to her little pallet bed and sat. She opened her chest, and took out the length of blue Azurro-dyed cloth. She lifted it to her face, remembering the night Bark had given it to her. Next, she pulled out her green Notary's costume. The thought that she must put it on forced her to consider the reality of her situation.

After what Dainty had said, the arguments had been going round and round in her head ever since. How would she manage? She'd lose her position, she'd be an outcast. Here she was, the first young woman to be so highly promoted and she was going to confirm all the men's prejudices: women were weak vessels, undereducated and prey to their emotions and their bodies. She looked down at her stomach - it didn't show anything, but how long before it gave her away? Her breasts were beginning to feel tender, she was still being sick, though she tried to be more discreet about it. Yet she couldn't rid herself of the thought that this was a little person, a real child, and Bark was its father. How could she kill that bit of him?

But whatever her heart felt, her head told her otherwise.

She went to find Lilac.

'Braymer's been sighted my Lady.'

Lilac was sitting reading a document.

'Ah, then we shall be docking in a day's time.' She scrutinised Ren. 'You'll be glad I expect, Ren. No more sickness.'

'Yes, I'm better already,' she lied.

'Good. We've plenty to do. I'm just reading through our plans.' She looked down at the document.

Ren stared at Lilac: her dark hair neat, tied back, her pale skin luminous against her lavender skirt and jacket. She was beautiful. Not for the first time, Ren was stung by jealousy.

'My Lady.' Ren hesitated, wanting to tell Lilac, to shatter her calm composure, her assumptions about Ren and Bark, to be rid of this secret eating away inside. Lilac looked up at her. Ren blushed under that look, and knew she wouldn't do it, she couldn't, not now, not yet. Instead she asked:

'How can we discuss this new dye with Braymer if we don't know for certain we'll get it?'

Lilac tapped the document: 'That's a possibility we must consider.'

'What if the Samarans sell it to another country?'

'Our industry is sophisticated. No-one produces blue like ours. It makes sense for them to trade with us. Bark himself said so.'

There was an awkward silence as his name hung in the air.

'Right. So Ren, get your green gown of office ready. You'll need to get used to wearing it.'

Ren nodded, determined not to let her feelings interfere

with her role as Notary to the Minister for Azurro. She still had time to sort out her problem.

That night, anxious and restless, she went to get fresh air on deck. She heard murmuring and a cooing, soft feathers flapping. In the starlit dark, she made out Charlatan releasing a bird from the side of the boat. She tiptoed back to bed.

It was Ren's first sight of a foreign country. The land undulated brown and green with a coastline that stretched in both directions as far as she could see. The water was a dull mud colour. As they came close to the port, the sails were reefed and smaller rowing boats tugged them into a harbour murky with bits of wood and rubbish, including a dead rat or two. She was disappointed by its dirty dishwater smell, nothing like the salty tang of the sea round Calico. There was a rush of bodies around her as the sailors busied themselves with ropes and baggage, preparing to draw up and moor at a bustling quayside.

Her head spinning, she stepped off the gangplank and was enveloped in earthy, sweaty bodies, and sickly sweet perfume. The solid ground still seemed to be moving. She feared she would vomit onto the foot of the Chancellor of Braymer: a portly red-faced man in a fur trimmed coat, who came in person to take them to the Chancellery in his carriage.

'Welcome, Lady Lilac. Beautiful as ever.' He kissed her hand.

'And you are her Notary?' He smiled at Ren: 'You are most welcome to Braymer. Excuse me.' He moved away and waved to Charlatan. They clasped hands, heads together, and had a short conversation. As Ren sat waiting while they loaded the bags, Dainty appeared at her side:

'Come and visit me at the Playhouse.'

Ren grabbed his hand: 'Don't forget your promise.'

The Chancellor returned: 'All ready?' He swept them up into his carriage: 'Drive on.'

Their driver flicked the reins and they lurched forward.

As they drove away, Ren turned to watch the actors - her last view was of Dainty leading a skittery blindfolded Dobbin down the gangplank to the safety of the quayside.

Ren was given a chamber next to Lilac's. It had a bed covered in many blankets and a rich tapestry hanging on the wall.

'My Lady, this is so grand.'

'This is not just a display of wealth, it's a practical measure. Braymer houses are draughty places.'

There was also a chair and small desk with inkstand: Ren touched the smooth wood, which smelled of beeswax, and stroked the feathers on the quill. She loved the calm space - it was her own, for writing.

That evening they dined with the Chancellor in his private rooms, a small party. There were silver candelabra lighting the table and crystal goblets, though he apologised for the 'homely affair' he offered. The heavy red liquor he insisted they drank gave Ren a muddled head. She was aware that Lilac and the Chancellor were talking seriously, something about a letter and the Governor of Calico. The Chancellor patted Lilac's arm in reassurance, and said:

'But of course, you are both welcome here, my dear.'

Ren wondered what he meant, but she was so weary she could hardly stop her head drooping into her game soup. She finally escaped to her bed. Although there was a bed-warmer, hot with coals, it had a smell of damp. She climbed in, glad to be rid of stirring water beneath her and fell into a deep sleep.

The next morning she was woken by the churning in her stomach and leapt up to be sick into a little pot she found under the bed. She wiped her brow, cold and clammy and pushed the pot back under the bed; she didn't know what else to do with it. Dressed in a pink gown, with tidied hair, she managed to look presentable. A maid knocked, telling her it was time for breakfast.

'Oh, thank you. I, er, I have.. I was not well this morning. The pot. Under the bed.' She felt ashamed but desperate, and blushed as she pointed.

'Not to worry, my Lady.'

Ren thanked her. A month ago, she'd been performing such duties. And a few months before that, she'd been a Blue Hand. Now she was being called 'my Lady'. She couldn't get used to it.

Breakfast was taken very seriously. It was considered an important meal in the day, with numbers of dishes to choose from: smoked fish and eggs, sausages and blood pudding. She couldn't hope to eat it safely, so she drank some peppermint tea and ate a little bread with jam, to the disappointment of the Chancellor.

'You will not see finer fare anywhere on Braymer, I guarantee.'

Lilac came to her rescue:

'It's not the quality of your food, dear sir. She's not used to such quantities.'

'We'll fatten you up and send you home singing the praises of our meat, see if we don't.' He tucked into a large plateful and drank glasses of spiced wine. Ren wondered if everyone in Braymer ate so much.

After breakfast they were given a tour of the port and wider city in the Chancellor's carriage. He and Lilac talked of this and that. Ren looked about, trying to remember the sights so she could describe her impressions to those at home.

Braymer Port rose back up into a ring of low hills cut through by the river. There were grey stone buildings and hundreds of smaller wooden houses all higgledy piggledy as if built by a child, tilting up in every available space. She'd never experienced a big bustling city. Horse-drawn carriages and carts rolled through the crowds, their drivers cracking whips, shouting to clear the way. Sailors and warehousemen were unloading cargoes with crashes and thumps. There were pens of bleating sheep, awaiting transportation on flat barges. Dogs barked, wheels racketed on cobbles, people were calling and hurrying about. It seemed a kind of madness. Some boats on the water had striped awnings, and their owners were shouting names and numbers:

'Far Resting Two ten! Marsh Flats six a penny!'

The Chancellor described them as public carriages; travellers could pay to be taken up river or across the harbour. Round the port, many of the larger buildings flew patterned flags or hung painted boards outside. These marked the theatre and cockpit, bathhouse and 'other such places of entertainments' the Chancellor explained.

It was easy to tell by signs what shops offered. A fish or pig for fishmonger or butcher, a steaming cup and a pipe for the coffee houses. They stopped beside a round wooden building many storeys high. Outside hung the Chancellor's coat of arms:

'My Playhouse!' he declared, 'where you shall witness the glories of our art and poesy. Do you enjoy the theatre?' he leant over to Ren and grinned.

'Yes, very much. Though on Calico I've only seen your men perform on their travelling cart.'

'Oh, you have a treat in store. Drive on!'

'Yes, the May Day revels caused quite a stir,' Lilac said. 'My father The Governor was most upset he was the subject of their comedy.'

The Chancellor chuckled: 'Big men must have broad backs.' He turned to Lilac and lowered his voice, 'The same goes for important women.'

'I think mine is broad enough,' she replied.

The Chancellor sighed: 'Good. You'll have to work hard to convince them that the new dye would work better than Shebble.'

Ren said: 'We'll tell them the new methods are safer for the Gild members!'

'I think you'll find they're only moved by profit.' The Chancellor smiled at her.

'Our profit figures are only guesses, sire.'

'Informed Estimates, Ren,' Lilac corrected her, 'I won't have any man say I was unprepared. We must be businesslike in the face of hostility.' Lilac looked determined.

'Hostility?' Ren queried. 'Who from?'

'It may be just rumour,' the Chancellor said, 'but I've heard that some are bent on destroying the success of your mission.'

'Do you think they use spies, like Grist?' Ren wondered, remembering Charlatan and the bird in the dark.

The Chancellor and Lilac exchanged a look.

Ren and the Blue Hands - Interview questions about the process

What inspired you to write Ren and the Blue Hands?

First of all, years ago, I came up with a scene and a character in a writing workshop. A young woman finding a secret note. It seemed to be about a mystery and I kept writing scenes - I wrote about young women working together in a dark shed and singing beautifully. I imagined a nasty villain when I was given the word Grist. So it all began with bits and pieces, and all seemed set in some historical past.

Then I read about the real struggle in the Dye industry in the 16th century, when the Guilds in Europe were resisting a new dye, Indigo, coming in from India. They called it the Devil's Dye - and that became the core of the story that pulled all my disparate bits of scenes and characters together. My women workers in a shed were Dyers, the Blue Hands. But I knew their resistance to the new dye was bound to failure, so I began to think about when change is inevitable, how and why do people adapt? I gave these dilemmas to my main character Ren, who's caught up in the middle of these big historical changes, and has to deal with it on a personal level.

You call it an alternative 16th Century, so is it fantasy?

No, because it's based on real events and all the technology and clothes are based on 16th life, but I've taken liberties with reality, and have created my own alternative world. I'm aiming for emotional rather than literal truth. It makes the book difficult to categorise by genre - it's a historical drama, but fictional, some call it fantasy because I made up the country, but that suggests dragons and elves - there's no magic or non-human characters. There's a love story at its heart, so it's a romance too, but it's also about political struggle. Try and sum up that in three words!

Did you have to do research?

I used many historical sources for help and ideas. It's been the greatest fun imaginable making up the world, my 16th Century cosmos. Characters have natural names like Bark and Moss and Count Saffron. The blue dye comes from the Shebble Shell. The group of isles where Shebble shell is found are The Calico Isles where the story is set. Braymer is the country that exports the wool and yarn that gets dyed by Shebble shell. The workers on Calico are organised by their Gild. The different classes of society are subject to sumptuary laws (which were real laws detailing who could wear what fabric and colour of clothing) - in my world only the wealthiest nobles are allowed to wear the unique Shebble blue dyed cloth, while workers in the dye industry get Blue Lung or Shebble Pox, and their hands are stained blue.

I'd done an MA in Theatre Studies, and had explored the traditions of Shakespearean theatre, so I included a Travelling Theatre troupe called The Chancellor of Braymer's Men who come to Calico to perform for the May Day Revels and stir things up. In the past there have been Dye Wars. The time of peaceful monopoly of Shebble is about to change.

Where is it set?

In my imagination, the Calico Isles are a combination of Mediterranean islands with elements of Cornwall. The country of Braymer is a colder, more northerly island, not a million miles away from Britain. Samara, the third major country referred to, is a mash-up of North African/Middle Eastern countries.

Was it a long process?

Yes!

I've been writing the story off and on for about 10 years, and it's only in the last four or five years that I really got down to working out how the story fitted together, and filling it out. It took two more books to get the story to a satisfactory end and I still haven't quite finished the third although I know where it's going. I haven't decided on the actual fate of my main character in the final chapter!

I put an early draft in for the Times / Chicken House Children's Novel competition in 2012 and it was long-listed which gave me a confidence boost, and encouraged me to keep working and finish it all.

Who are your favourite YA authors?

Two of my favourites are Ursula Le Guin, particularly The Wizard of Earthsea, and the Chaos Walking trilogy by Patrick Ness. Not only are they great writers of stories that you can't put down, but they also explore real, serious issues that people have to deal with: moral dilemmas, how to choose the right decision in difficult circumstances, with complex characters who are both good and bad. They set their stories in other worlds, but that allows the reader to reflect back on the real world. If I could achieve that in my writing, I'd be happy.

Acknowledgements

This has been a long journey - I owe a huge debt to Jane Wood, Judy Walker and Tessa Green who tirelessly read, reread, commented and encouraged me all the way. Many others helped and advised, so I want to thank: New Writing North, Debbie Taylor and The Fast Track Novel Group; Helen Limon for her patient and insightful readings of many drafts; The Folk Book Group, Eleanor Cobb, Meg Pinfield and Phoebe Walker for reading and commenting on early drafts; The Writing for Children group for inspiration over the years. Tessa Green for the cover design. Judy Walker for proof reading. The Lit and Phil Library and Kay Easson, Librarian, for her generosity and creative energy. Sheila Wakefield, Founder Editor, Red Squirrel Press, as ever, for her support and belief in her drey of writers.

I particularly want to thank Sarah Hosking and the Hosking Houses Trust for the residency and financial support allowing me to work on the novel undisturbed February - March 2016. A room of my own just when I needed it.

www.hoskinghouses.co.uk

An early draft was long listed for the Times/Chicken House Children's fiction Competition 2012.

The novel began many years ago and was inspired by

actual historical events, but I've taken liberties with reality, and have created my own world. I'm aiming for emotional rather than literal truth. However, I did use many sources for help and ideas. Please see below for some further reading.

Ellen's website: www.diamondtwig.co.uk
Tweets as @phethean

Bibliography

Indigo: In search of the colour that seduced the world
- Catherine McKinley, Bloomsbury 2011

Her Majesty's Spymaster
- Stephen Budiansky, Plume 2006

This Orient Isle
- Jerry Brotton, Allen Lane, 2016

Life in Renaissance Europe
- Sandra Sider, OUP, 2007

*Vermeer's Hat, The Seventeenth Century
and the Dawn of the Global World*
- Timothy Brook, Profile Books, 2009

Pirates and Privateers, The History of Maritime Piracy
- http://www.cindyvallar.com/medicine.html

The Travels of Marco Polo
- Edited with an Introduction by Manuel Komroff, Liveright
Publishing Corp.

http://www.elizabethan.org/sumptuary/who-wears-what.
html - Sumptuary Laws